HUNTER

The Silver Series: Book 6

By Cheree L. Alsop

HUNTER

Copyright © 2013 by Cheree L. Alsop
All rights reserved. This book or any portion thereof may not be reproduced or used in any manner whatsoever without the express written permission of the author except for the use of brief quotations in a book review.

This is a work of fiction. Names, characters, places, and incidents are a product of the author's imagination. Any resemblance to actual persons, events, or locales is entirely coincidental.

ISBN 9781482009361

Cover Design by Andy Hair

www.ChereeAlsop.com

CHEREE ALSOP

To my husband, Michael Alsop,
Whose love of a farm girl
Made all my dreams come true.

To my children for every new
Adventure. Life through a
Child's eyes makes every
Day a new beginning.

I love you!

HUNTER

Chapter 1

My old green truck shuddered like a wet cat when I shifted into first. The lights of the railroad crossing flashed dull red against the dusty horizon. I tried to find something other than country on the radio, but station pickings were slim and country hearts rang true in these parts. A small thud sounded in front of me. I sighed and glanced up, then frowned.

The Harrison's yellow car sat halfway across the tracks. The sound had been the wooden arm of the railroad crossing hitting the back of their car. The brake lights flashed and I could see Mrs. Harrison's head bobbing frantically in the front seat. A horn sounded. My heart skipped a beat at the sight of the nightly train rushing its passengers back from the city.

I jumped out of the truck and ran to Mrs. Harrison's window. "What's going on?" I demanded.

"It died," she shouted through the glass. She gestured toward the back seat, her eyes wide with fright. I followed her gaze to Peggy and baby John asleep in their car seats. The ignition clicked when she tried desperately to turn the car back on.

The train charged down the tracks. There wasn't time for me to get both children from the car seats. My heart pounded in my chest. On impulse, I ran to the front of the car. Unsure of what else to do, I grabbed the bumper and pulled as hard as I could. The metal bit into my hands, the cold a stark contrast to the fire of fear that raced through my body when the car didn't move. I gritted my teeth and pulled again.

The car slid grudgingly forward. The horn of the train called once more, so close this time it reverberated through the metal of the car and up my arms. I shut my eyes, said a silent prayer, and pulled with all of the strength I had. I moved back slowly one step at a time. My brain screamed that it was too slow, but I couldn't give up. I felt the back tires bump over the first rail. The entire car shook with the force of the train barreling toward us.

I gave one last pull, then tripped over backwards as the back tires cleared the second rail and rolled down the decline from the tracks. The train screamed by, its brakes screeching so loud my ears felt shredded by the sound. I stood up slowly, my arms and legs trembling. When I met Mrs. Harrison's amazed gaze, I realized what I had just done.

The train slowed. Too anxious to wait for it to stop and worried that others would show up and make me explain myself, I followed the gaps and jumped across the next opening. I jogged to my truck and breathed a sigh of relief when it started on the first try. I backed up and took the long way down the tracks and across, then up past the Morris fields to our house.

I pulled the truck into the shed that leaned as though it would fall down any minute but had looked the same way for the last five years since I hit it with Dad's combine. I sat still, thinking about what had happened. I wondered if it looked a little too unbelievable from an outsider's point of view; it definitely had from mine. I pushed my sun-worn brown cowboy hat back from my forehead, vaguely surprised that it had stayed on. Sweat trickled into my eyes and I rubbed it away with the back of my arm, then stared at the beads of moisture across my skin.

I never sweat. Even in the middle of summer when we spent the days shucking hay or burning ditches, I still came home in a dry tee-shirt. Mom said it was a gift, but we knew the truth. I was different, more different than the little town of Thistle could handle.

I climbed out of the truck, patted its rusted green hood, then left through the back door of the shed. I followed the worn rut across the grass to the barn. The steady shoosh-shoosh from the open door announced that Dad was already milking our four cows. I climbed the wooden ladder to the rafters and pitched hay into the feeders. I used to do the milking, but the cows had become increasingly distrustful of me and I couldn't blame them. Dad and I switched jobs and I preferred the humid loft and the dry, sweet smell of hay to moody cows that kicked at me whenever I went near them.

I sat and let my feet dangle over the edge. The cows munched contentedly below, and the familiar sounds of Dad pouring milk into the strainer along with the occasional stomp of a hoof and the faint buzz of the always-present flies chased away some of the anxiety in my chest. I chewed on a piece of hay to calm my nerves; the sweet green taste filled me with a longing for rolling fields and simple skies without trains, cars, or people in trouble.

"How was your day?" Dad called up.

I settled my hat more firmly on my head and pushed myself over the edge to land softly on the ground. The drop was a good fifteen feet, but I barely felt it. Dad lifted an eyebrow. His jeans had grass stains on the knees that Mom could never get out, he wore the red checkered shirt I had given him for Christmas, and his black hat had faded to dark gray with a sweat stain around the band. He pulled a handkerchief from his pocket and rubbed the barnyard grime from his hands.

"I take it you had a rough one?" he guessed.

I took off my hat and ran a hand through my sweaty sun-blond hair. Dad's eyes took in the sweat, but he had a farmer's patience and chose to wait for me to explain. I took a calming breath, then dropped my eyes. "I pulled a car from the train tracks by the Murphy place."

"Did anyone see you?" his calm voice held an undertone of worry.

I nodded. "Mrs. Harrison was in the car with Peggy and baby John. There was the train driver, and I didn't wait around to see if anyone else witnessed it."

He was silent for a moment and I looked up to see his gaze distant and his eyebrows pulled low over his light blue eyes. "Let's go talk to Ma," he concluded.

I followed him silently to the house and set my boots on the bench by the door. Jo, the border collie puppy Dad had bought from the Wilsons, ran through the door before it could shut. He tripped over Dad's work boot and sprawled into the wall. The puppy yipped at the boot, then tumbled through the door after Dad. I put the boot back by Dad's other one, hung my hat on a peg, then followed them slowly down the hall.

I paused by the door and my stomach growled at the scent of Mom's warm apple cobbler and fresh baked bread. I could hear them already talking. I sighed and put my forehead against the wall. Years of Mom's cooking, the faint scent of the barnyard, and the smell of the wood burning stove in our small living room had imprinted in the wood and fading yellow wallpaper. The smell was as familiar to me as alfalfa under my fingers. I held in a breath and let it out slowly, then focused on their conversation.

"If she tells the police what really happened, we might have some explaining to do," Dad said, his voice heavy with worry.

"Maybe it'll wash over and we won't hear anything," Mom replied calmly. She wiped her hands on a rag and hung it over the cupboard door. It gave a slight squeak when she pushed it closed.

"We need to plan for the worst. What if we have to send him away?"

Mom's reply was stern but gentle. "Jason, dear, there's nowhere for him to go. He's our son and I'm not sending him anywhere."

"What if he's not safe here?"

My heart clenched at the question I had heard them both discuss more often as my differences became further pronounced. I didn't want to leave home, but I didn't want to worry them. Sometimes I felt so guilty at the trouble I caused even when I didn't mean to that I debated running away; but I could never leave Dad with all the farm work, and I knew it would break Mom's heart.

I stepped into the kitchen. "Is that pie I smell?"

They both looked up quickly from the table, then exchanged a glance that asked if I had overheard. I pretended not to notice. "Mom, you always bake the best apple pies. You really should enter them in the Fair this year."

Mom stood up with her modest smile. "Oh, Dray. It's just apples and crust. Nothing special."

"Tell that to Jo," I said, indicating the puppy that waited in front of the oven, his white-tipped tail waving and his nose high.

She laughed and shooed him out of the kitchen. "If Jo was the judge, then I'd enter."

Dad rose from the table and helped Mom carry over a chicken and peas casserole, fresh slices of bread that steamed as they cooled, a jar of Mom's raspberry preserves, and a glass pitcher of fresh milk. I set the plates at the table and aligned the silverware neatly with the dishes.

Mom often said that while we lived on a farm, we would eat like civilized folk, although I never could figure out why living on a farm meant we weren't civilized. I asked her once and she said with a laugh that we spent too much time with animals and not enough time socializing, so she kicked us out of the house once in a while so she could have her ladies over for gossiping and cards.

We sat at the table and ate, careful not to talk about the train or Mrs. Harrison's possible reactions. I spread butter on the bread and watched it melt almost immediately, soaking into the center and making it soft and damp just the way I liked it. I spread the preserves on top and relished the taste of Mom's cooking.

"Did you see Henry's new foal?" Dad asked.

"I haven't," Mom replied.

I shook my head.

Dad put his elbows on the table; at Mom's look, he took them back down and gestured with his hands. "It's black and white with four white socks, a stripe down its nose, and a patch on its right side that looks just like a rabbit. Ears up and everything. The horse's sire was a dun. Henry's puzzled over the whole thing."

I smiled at his enthusiasm and took a bite of the casserole. "Did they name it Bugs?"

Mom looked puzzled for a minute, then laughed. "Bugs Bunny. That would be a great name for it."

Dad smiled. "I'll have to mention it to them."

"Will you really?" I couldn't picture Dad suggesting for another farmer to name his horse after a cartoon rabbit.

He shook his head. "Not a chance."

Mom and I laughed and we finished our meal with small talk about the farm and Mom's continued efforts to make a pie better than Mildred Cottonward's who won all the blue ribbons at the Fair. Vanilla bean ice cream melted around Mom's fresh apple cobbler, making the perfect balance between the almost too hot to eat apples and the cold ice cream. I traced patterns through the melted cream with my fork; my mind flashed back to the train, wondering if the wreckage would have looked much the same way if I hadn't been there.

"Dray?"

I realized Mom had repeated my name several times and looked up. "Yeah?"

She threw Dad a light glance, concern in her eyes. "I was just wondering if you're going to the game tomorrow night."

I sighed. "I suppose. I don't think Preston will let me live it down if I miss it." While the thought of watching one of my few friends run around the football field dressed like a giant ear of corn didn't exactly sound like the height of fun, it was something to do besides sitting at home.

"We're going, too," Mom said. She gave me a reassuring smile. "But we'll sit in the parent section so we don't embarrass you."

They went to every game like every single person in Thistle, so I wasn't surprised. "You don't embarrass me," I said, as much because they wanted to hear it as because it was true.

"Well, just the same we'll be sitting with Mabel and Stan in our usual seats."

"I have to study after school, so I'll probably just meet you there."

Dad was about to say something when a knock sounded at the door.

"Hello?" It was Mrs. Harrison; her soft, high voice carried a faint note of anxiety. My heart fell.

"Go to the barn," Mom whispered. "We'll tell her you're out with Preston."

I slipped out the back door, catching the screen so it didn't slam shut behind me. I was tempted to listen in on the conversation, but realized I didn't really want to know what Mrs. Harrison would say. I walked across the short lawn Mom kept carefully manicured and stepped over the railroad ties that marked the end of the lawn and the beginning of the dirt road that circled the barn and led down through our fields.

I kicked a rock and watched the dust rise briefly in the twilight before being whisked away by the faint evening breeze. I circled around to the back of the barn and leaned against the rough wooden wall. I breathed in deeply through my nose. My brain categorized the scent of the alfalfa that swayed under the waxing moon and looked like a living ocean touched with dark green and faint brushes of purple where flowers would soon open to the bees. The brackish scent of the slow-moving Tayne River less than a mile away brought with it the faint sound of frogs singing their chorus to the night. In the barn behind me a cow stomped and chewed its cud lazily.

The urge to run through the fields rushed within my limbs. I closed my fingers convulsively into fists, driving away the want to change, to become something I couldn't explain, something that set me apart from everyone else in Thistle and that I feared would eventually make me have to leave.

I never told Mom and Dad how I felt. They knew I was different. They had been there during my first change and even though we couldn't explain it, they were there for every full moon, keeping me safe and making sure no one found out my secret. But if I ever became dangerous, or got to the point where my differences put them in a tough position, I would leave to protect them.

The screen door opened and Jo's paws pattered across the dirt followed by Dad's measured footsteps. The puppy charged around the side of the barn and I crouched to meet him. He practically flew into my arms, then licked my chin and cheeks with his long pink tongue until I pushed him back down.

"Need a shower now?" Dad asked with a touch of a smile.

"Just had one," I answered, petting Jo's soft head. I stood and shoved my hands into my pockets. "So what'd she say?"

Dad's eyes creased slightly at the corners and I was surprised to hear pride in his voice when he said, "That you saved her, Peggy, and baby John from the train. That if it wasn't for you, they'd all be dead right now. Sam was with them."

Sam and Dad had a mild rivalry when it came to selling hay. They met sometimes at the one bar in town and ribbed each other about the prices they got from the dairy farmers. Dad's tone was funny when he said Sam's name and I glanced up to see his eyes shining in the moonlight. "Sam hugged me and thanked me for having such a great kid."

"They didn't, uh, say anything about how pulling a car off the tracks should be impossible?" I asked with a pit in my stomach.

He shook his head. "Nothing of the sort." He glanced at me and ruffled my hair in the way he knew I hated. "I think we're okay."

Relief lifted a heavy weight from my shoulders. I closed my eyes and leaned back against the rough wooden wall. "I wasn't thinking, Dad. I just-"

He squeezed my shoulder and waited until I opened my eyes again. "You acted, and you saved lives. I'm proud of you." His tone changed and light danced in his gaze. "She brought you something."

"What is it?" I asked cautiously.

He walked toward the house and left me to follow. I took

a steeling breath and stepped through the moonlight to our back door. The moon played along my hair and a shudder ran across my skin, a memory of running through fields on four swift paws, of startling killdeer and ducks at the edge of the river, of loping with my nose in the wind, the moonlight on my fur, and soft earth under my paws tangled my thoughts. I ran both hands roughly through my hair to chase away the feeing and opened the door.

I found Mom and Dad in the front room. A scent touched my nose before I saw the little black ball sitting on Mom's lap.

"A cat?" I asked in disbelief.

"A kitten," Mom corrected with laughter in her eyes. "Mrs. Harrison brought it as a thank you gift."

"I'm not exactly a cat person," I said, but the soft, long black hair beckoned to be petted. I moved to touch it when the kitten smelled me. It arched its back and hissed, its tongue pink and teeth very white against its black fur. I backed up quickly. "I guess the feeling's mutual," I said.

Mom let out a small, apologetic laugh. "I'll take it back in the morning."

But her hand lingered on its fur, smoothing it down until the kitten curled back in her lap, its orange eyes on my face. "You keep it," I suggested. "It seems to like you."

She shook her head. "I won't have you two chasing each other around the house."

Dad and I both stared at her. After a second, laughter began bubbling from Dad like a leaky hose. Dad seldom laughed, but when he did, it was so contagious you couldn't help but join in. The three of us laughed until our sides hurt and the kitten moved out of Mom's lap and curled up next to the stove in protest.

Chapter 2

I parked my truck next to Sherrie's bright red Neon. The truck shuddered to a stop and I climbed out, pulling my black backpack off the seat and slinging it over one shoulder. I shut the door, but didn't bother to lock it. There wasn't anything inside worth stealing, and if they tried to steal the truck, I doubted they would get it started with the stubborn clutch.

Scotty, a tall, skinny boy with black hair and the confidence of a movie star pulled up next to my truck in his vintage Charger. "When you gonna trade that thing in for a real car?" he asked when he got out, careful to keep his letterman's jacket from touching my truck.

I rolled my eyes. "When cows fly. My truck works just fine."

He eyed it suspiciously. "Bring it by the lot. Dad'll give you a good price on a trade, even though it can't be worth much."

I stifled a sigh. "I appreciate the offer, but I like my truck. It has character."

"You mean character like a slug, or a turtle." Scotty pointed at his car, lost to the fact that I was no longer paying attention. "What you need is character like four hundred and twenty-five horses barreling down the road. That kind of character gets you girls."

We walked toward the school and I glanced back. "I don't see them lining up."

He shoved my shoulder and laughed. "They are, trust me." Then he paused. "By the way, I heard what you did at the tracks, good job."

My stomach tightened. "What are you talking about?"

He grinned. "My dad read in the paper this morning how you helped Mrs. Harrison."

I rubbed my eyes and debated whether to take a sick day, but if it was in the news, it was too late to avoid. I shoved my hands in my pockets and sighed. "They probably exaggerated the details. You know how the news is."

Scotty nodded as though this confirmed his suspicions. "They made it sound like you pulled the entire car over the tracks by yourself. I figured there was more to it than that."

"Definitely," I agreed casually without expounding.

We were almost to the doors when a light scent teased my nose. The scent was female and carried an aroma of sunshine and strawberries, but there was an underlying smell I didn't recognize. I turned to find the source, and saw a girl walking with her parents toward the doors on the far end of the building.

She had bright pink hair in a pixie cut and wore a light blue long-sleeved shirt and skinny pants that flared at the ankle to reveal silver sneakers. She smiled and skipped around on her tiptoes in front of her parents as they followed her inside. They both wore matching expressions of uncertainty, but the girl beamed with confidence and excitement as she led them through the door.

"Uh, Dray? Earth to Dray?"

I looked back to see Scotty standing with the door open waiting for me to come inside. I glanced back one last time, but the girl was gone. The bell rang and Scotty and I raced for class.

We did a review in American History for the test on Friday. I took notes, but Scotty's comment that the story was in the news kept running through my mind. I wondered what Mrs. Harrison had told them, and hoped it was hidden somewhere in the paper where few people would notice.

My hopes fell when Mr. Andrews called me to his desk just after the bell rang. "Yes, sir?"

He set the Thistle Times down on his desk and pointed to the front page where Mrs. Harrison stood next to her car, the train tracks in the background. "I just wanted to thank you for being so brave."

I dropped my eyes. "It was nothing, sir. I just happened to be in the right place at the right time."

"You can say that again," Mr. Andrews said with a warm smile. "Mrs. Harrison is my neighbor, and I'm glad she and the kids are alright."

"Me, too," I replied, trying to sound positive.

A pause followed, then Mr. Andrews cleared his throat. "You'd better get to your next class before you're late."

"Thank you, sir," I said. I left quickly and rushed into Sophomore English just before the bell rang.

A scent stopped me inside the door and I looked up to see the girl with pink hair standing next to Mrs. Moody. She watched me with blue eyes that sparkled to match the smile on her lips. I caught myself staring and walked quickly to my desk. The bell rang as I sat down; I pretended to be busy locating my book in my backpack.

"Class, I'd like you to meet Gem Hawthorne." There were a few mumbled hellos, but no one was sociable in morning English. It passed like American History, quick, but full of facts I missed because I was too busy worrying about the story in the paper. I wondered if Mom and Dad had seen it, and hoped they weren't getting bombarded with questions.

Gem sat on the other side of the classroom, but her scent still carried to me above the rest and I stole glances in her direction. It unnerved me when on the third time I found her looking back. Her nose crinkled slightly when she smiled; my cheeks burned and I looked away. I stared unseeing at the book on my desk for several minutes, but when I glanced back she was still watching me with the cute smile that unnerved me down to my bones.

I hurried out of class when the bell rang and met Preston and Scotty on the way to gym. Preston was six foot four, but he was too skinny for the football team and couldn't dribble to save his life, so he had been given the position of the mascot. He said he enjoyed it because it got him close to the cheerleaders, but he had yet to actually talk to one.

"So when you're not farming, you're pulling cars from train tracks?" he asked in an off-hand way as we changed and lined up for roll.

I noticed several other classmates listening in and tried to switch subjects. "The new crop's almost ready for harvest, so I might miss the game tonight."

They both stared at me. "You're just saying that," Scotty finally decided. "You did something heroic and hate the fame that comes with it. You're going to have to face it sometime."

"You wouldn't miss the game to cut hay, would you?" Preston asked in shock, still stuck on the matter.

Scotty shook his head. "No one misses the game. He's bluffing."

"You're bluffing, right?" Preston pressed.

I finally sighed and nodded. "I'll be there."

Preston grinned in relief. "I'm trying a new move I've been working on with the cheerleaders." He waited for us to comment; when we didn't, he nudged me with his elbow. "Did you hear that? New move with the cheerleaders?"

"I heard." I tried to picture Preston putting actual moves on any cheerleader while dressed as the giant ear of corn and found myself feeling better.

Preston took my smile to mean I agreed he had a possibility with the girls and shot a triumphant look at Scotty. "It's a good plan."

Scotty rolled his eyes and patted his carefully styled hair

to make sure none of the strands had moved out of place when he changed. "If you get a phone number, let me know."

Preston's reply was cut off when Coach Matthews walked into the gymnasium. "Give me twenty laps, ladies."

Everyone grumbled, but began to jog around the painted rectangle that outlined the basketball court.

"Mr. Dawson, come talk to me," he called over the sound of twenty-five pairs of feet hitting the wooden gym floor.

"What now?" I asked Scotty. He shrugged. I dropped off halfway through the lap and jogged over to where Coach Matthews sat on the bottom bench of the stands making notes on a clipboard.

He glanced up when I neared and motioned for me to sit next to him. He was silent for several moments, then pointed at the students. "What do you see there?"

I studied them running around the gym, some goofing off, others determined to get their laps done so they could rest, and a few stragglers, Scotty included because he hated to break a sweat, bringing up the rear at a leisurely pace. "Um, students," I said, wondering what answer he was looking for.

"Slackers," the Coach said with an explosiveness that sent a rush of fight or flight adrenaline through my veins. I let out a slow breath and felt the urge to defend myself fade. The Coach didn't notice. "They have no heart. Look at them!"

I looked and even though he was right, I didn't want to talk bad about guys I had grown up with; I considered most of them friends or at least acquaintances.

Coach Matthews frowned and glared at the clipboard. "What I need is a kicker." He glanced at me and the familiar pit formed in my stomach. "I need someone with heart I can count on, someone strong who can be relied on in tough situations, who can act the hero when needed."

I gritted my teeth. "Are you referring to the train incident by any chance?"

His eyes lit up. "Exactly! I need someone who can pull a car from the tracks when we're in trouble." His voice dropped conspiratorially. "And the football team this year isn't exactly in the clear if you know what I mean."

I thought of their last three wins and shook my head. "I don't think I do."

Several of the students had finished their laps and lounged against the far wall; a few lay dramatically exhausted on the ground, while some lined up by the drinking fountain. Coach Matthews seemed not to notice. He lifted a sheet of paper and pointed to the roster of his team. "Jamison's got a scholarship to the U next year, so we're out the best quarterback we've ever had. Johnson, my second string, can barely throw ten yards, and there're no good freshmen candidates." He pulled the paper back down and I could see his mind working. He pursed his lips and his eyebrows drew together. "What I need is a kicker that I can train as a quarterback."

I tried to protest, but he cut me off. "I know it doesn't make sense, but you've never played before and I really do need a kicker this year. Then Jamison can train you on off-time so you're ready for next year."

My chest tightened. I wanted more than anything to be part of the football team. It was a dream of mine, a way to get into college without costing Mom and Dad a fortune, a way to be part of a team, to wear a letterman jacket and hang out with the guys, going to parties and living the real high school life. But I knew better than anyone why I couldn't.

"I'm sorry, Coach," I said and watched his face fall. "I've got to help Dad on the farm. It's almost time to harvest again, then he'll need my help ripping and irrigating, and we need to prepare the fields for next spring-"

He shook his head with an impatient sigh. "Dray, I know you're right for this team, and I see how badly you want it. Why won't you just accept that you were made to play football?"

Because apparently I had been made for far different things that even I didn't know the half of. I searched for an appropriate answer and looked up to find that the entire class had wandered over. Scotty watched me with raised eyebrows and nodded encouragingly, while Preston grinned and shrugged, his red hair now sticking up in a million different directions from running.

Coach Matthews cleared his throat and they all jumped as if stung. "Get the baseball gear," he grumbled, eying them crossly. "Head out to the field." He turned back to me. "We'll talk later," he reassured in a voice that wasn't at all reassuring.

I nodded and grabbed a bat, then jogged out after the others.

HUNTER

***

"It's not like you couldn't do both," Scotty argued, gesturing emphatically with a french fry.

"I can't," I said for the hundredth time. "There's too much work to do on the farm and Dad can't handle it all."

"It's alright," Preston jumped to my defense and I gave him a grateful smile. "If football's not for him, he can take up sewing or something more fitting."

My smile turned to a glare and I focused my attention on my cold chicken sandwich which was actually quite good. The intriguing scent touched my nose again and I glanced over to see Gem sitting near one of the windows, sunlight playing across her tray as she fiddled with her spoon. She turned it just right and the light splashed me in the eyes. I blinked and she lowered the spoon, giving me an apologetic smile. Dimples showed in her cheeks and her teeth were straight and white. Someone spoke to her and she whispered something that sounded like, "Sorry about that, Dray," before she turned away.

I stared at her, wondering if my mind had made it up or I was going crazy. There was no way she could know of my freakishly sharp hearing, yet the words had sounded so clear, even whispered as they were. I frowned at my food and tried to decide if the stress of the spreading news about the train was making me go insane.

"You have a thing for the new girl?" Scotty guessed, following my gaze.

When I didn't answer, he laughed, "You don't have a chance with her."

Off-balanced by her smile, I turned to him. "What do you mean? She doesn't seem to be in a relationship."

"I don't mean nobody has a chance with her, I just mean *you* don't have a chance with her," he replied with his cocky smile. He checked his hair one more time to make sure it was in place, then rose and took his tray to her table.

I could only stare, jealous of his confidence. I felt like I should be the one talking to her. Protectiveness rose in my chest even though I didn't know anything about her; I just knew she could do better than both Scotty and I.

Scotty talked to her for a minute and it seemed like everything was going fine, then his shoulders stiffened and he rose and stalked back to our table, slamming his tray down when he sat.

"What happened?" Preston asked.

"She said she was behind so she had to commit to her studies, which wouldn't give her time for a boyfriend."

I stared at him. "You asked her to go out with you? You were only over there about two seconds."

He glared at me, then shrugged as if no longer bothered by her rejection. "I asked her if the sun ever got jealous of her beauty."

Preston and I both laughed at the line; Scotty ate a french fry and ignored us.

HUNTER

Chapter 3

I finished studying for my History test after school and started to pack up my stuff when my senses tingled; I looked up to see Gem enter the library. She had an armful of school books and looked around for somewhere to sit. When she spotted me, her eyes lit up and my heart did a funny flip in my chest. She crossed to my side and set her books on the table. "Are you leaving?" she asked, noticing my backpack.

I wanted to say no, but it was pretty obvious. "I was going to catch the football game. My friend, uh, Preston, is the, uh, mascot."

Her blue eyes sparkled. "You mean he's a corn grower? How does that work?"

I grinned. "He dresses like a giant ear of corn. It's hilarious really."

Her face took on a wistful expression. "That's something I'd like to see."

"You could come with me," I offered, my heart in my throat.

She looked like she was about to accept, then her gaze landed on the books she had just set down and her expression fell. "I've missed a bit of school," she explained, her tone strange and eyes down. "I have some catching up to do, so I'll have to take a rain check."

"Is there anything I can help you with?"

She shook her head and sat down. "It's just a lot of studying. You go enjoy the game." She opened a book, but stared at it as though she saw something else instead.

"Okay, well, um, have fun studying," I said, at a loss for anything else I could do. She didn't seem to notice me anymore, so I excused myself and left quietly. I glanced back once to see her head bowed over her book. Her pink hair stood out bright amid the tans and greens of the library, but her expression was so lost and distant I wanted to go back and do or say something that would make her feel better.

I finally left when I couldn't figure out what it was I should say. My heart twisted strangely in my chest at the thought of her sitting there so alone. I forced myself to cross the lawn to the outdoor stadium and the cheering that rose from the stands. A long line of people waited to get inside to watch the game.

I showed my student ID and got in free, then met up with several friends in the student section. I glanced around and saw Mom and Dad in the regular stands. Mom waved at me excitedly, then put a hand over her mouth as if remembering her promise not to embarrass me. She turned away and pointedly ignored me, but the next time I caught her looking my way I waved and she smiled.

The first half of the game went well. Scotty played running back and had several good carries, and Preston was in good form teasing the bullfrog mascot from the other team. My chest ached with every throw and Coach Matthews' words kept echoing in my head. I longed to say yes, to accept the position of kicker so I could train for quarterback. It was such a great opportunity, and passing it up hurt so badly I could barely stand to watch the game.

I studied the quarterback's form, his stance, the way he stepped into each throw. Jamison's spirals were tight, but the ones I threw through the old tire swing in our yard were tighter. I felt each release and searched for the receivers I would throw to, but I knew it was different from the field with the mad rush of the line wanting more than anything to smash the quarterback to the ground. I wondered how it felt to have only my wits and the skill of my team to protect me. I lost myself in the game and only realized after it was over that

HUNTER

I hadn't said a word to anyone the entire time.

I walked to my truck and found Mom and Dad waiting for me. "Dad wants to ride with you," Mom said before I could ask.

Mom and Dad never rode separately, let alone Mom driving after dark by choice. I decided not to ask and tossed Dad my keys. He caught them with a small smile and climbed onto the driver's seat. We waited until Mom pulled up in their maroon town car and followed her silently out of the parking lot.

"Good game," Dad said, his eyes scanning the road for deer. "It was close."

"I like them close. It makes it more exciting," I replied, my thoughts elsewhere.

"I think Coach Matthews would prefer to destroy them. It'd probably be better for his health."

I thought of the Coach pacing up and down the sideline, his clipboard clenched in one fist and the other one waving in the air. The current performance of his team determined whether the yells were positive or negative.

"I'm not sure it would make much of a difference; he shouts a lot either way," I replied.

Dad chuckled. "I suppose you're right."

We rode in comfortable silence for a few minutes, then Dad shattered it. "Stan mentioned a wolf killed two of his cows last night."

My heart froze and it took a moment for me to breathe again. "Wh-why would he say it was a wolf instead of a mountain lion or a coyote?"

Dad's eyes stayed on the road ahead of us. "The paw prints were too big to be a coyote, and there were claw marks, so he ruled out a cougar. He's positive it was a wolf." He glanced at me and I read the reluctant question in his eyes.

I shook my head emphatically, sick to my stomach that they thought I had anything to do with it. "I was home all night, I swear. I wouldn't-"

Dad held up a hand. "It's alright. Mom and I figured as much, I just had to ask."

"Did you?" I asked sullenly.

He was silently for a moment, then sighed and shook his head. "No, I guess not. We know you wouldn't do anything like that."

I sat back in my seat and stared out the side window. My mind raced with a new train of thoughts. "But who would?" A slight note of worry mixed with excitement in my voice.

This time, Dad took his full attention off the road and stared at me. "What are you saying?"

"What if there are other, well, you know, others like me out there?" The thought set a thrill of energy up my spine.

Dad turned back to the road, his eyes creasing with concern at the corners. "Dray, we've been through this. Your ma and I have looked everywhere and asked as many questions as we dared, but no one knows of anyone with your... condition."

I stared out the window and my eyes reflected back with a golden cast. The moon showed just above the horizon. It would be full in five days. I closed my eyes and turned forward. For lack of anything else to change the subject, I said, "Coach Matthews asked me to join the team."

A grunt of surprise came from Dad. "He did, did he?"

I nodded without opening my eyes. "He heard about the train incident."

"And thought someone strong enough to pull a car alone should be running a football?" Dad concluded.

"Kicking."

"What?" The surprise in Dad's voice made me smile.

I opened my eyes and looked at him. "He wanted me to start as a kicker so he could secretly train me to replace Jamison as quarterback next year."

A louder grunt of surprise came from Dad. "Quarterback, huh?" He glanced at me and I realized by his expression that he knew more of my dreams to play than I guessed. "What did you say?"

I tried not to sound bitter. "I told him I had to help my dad on the farm."

He fell silent for a few minutes, then let out a small chuckle. "He must think me quite the hypocrite if I won't let you play but we go to all the games."

A laugh broke from me at the thought. "Yeah, he must."

***

I sat two rows from Gem in English and noticed that she had as hard of a time paying attention to Macbeth as I did. She doodled on her notebook and I found myself wishing I could see what she drew. My gaze drifted from her page to where her sleeve had slipped back on her arm. She wore a long sleeved shirt and pants again despite the warmer than usual September weather. Most of the other students were taking advantage of the prolonged shorts and tee-shirt temperatures; it made Gem's clothing appear conservative by contrast.

A dark stripe showed across her arm. I frowned, studying it. It didn't look tattooed, but it was too dark to be pen or grease. It looked permanent, like-

Gem shoved her shirt sleeve back down and glared at me, her expression hurt. She gathered up her books and left the room despite the fact that Mrs. Moody was only halfway through the lecture. I stared after her, surprised by her strong reaction and feeling guilty at the same time like I had been caught doing something I shouldn't. I wanted to follow her, but the look Mrs. Moody gave the rest of the class after the door shut behind Gem threatened that anyone else who left wouldn't get off so easily.

I thought of the mark on Gem's arm through my next two classes and looked for Gem at lunch, but she was nowhere to be found.

"She didn't show up to Economics," Preston said when I finally broke down and asked him.

"Maybe she went home sick," Scotty guessed, his tone indicating he couldn't care less.

Whatever it was, I felt responsible and searched for her as I walked to each class, but I didn't see or smell her the rest of the day.

HUNTER

***

Dad was home when I got there, unusual considering the only time he ever stayed home was if someone died or he had pneumonia and Mom forced him to stay in bed. He met me at the door, a paper in his hand and a grim expression on his face. "Two more cows dead at the Murphy's, and four sheep from the Andersen's."

I grabbed the Thistle Times and stared at the gruesome cover picture depicting a beautiful fall day with four slaughtered sheep lying in a bed of green grass. "A little macabre for the front cover, don't you think?" I asked to cover up the alarm growing in my mind.

Dad frowned, his eyes on the picture. "The article says the farmers are taking action. They're going on a hunt."

I thought quickly. "The full moon's in four days. I can hide out until then. There's nothing to connect me to any of the killings."

Dad met my eyes, his own deadly serious. "It's not you I'm worried about."

"Then who?"

He nodded at the paper. "It says there are wolf tracks bigger than any wolf we've ever had in these parts. If these killings were caused by someone like you, then he's in trouble, big trouble, if the hunters catch him." His expression pinched with worry. "And you are, too, if anyone ever puts two and two together."

I swallowed the knot that rose in my throat. "We need to go with the hunters."

Dad's eyebrows rose. "What?"

I rushed on, "If we're there, maybe we can stop them before they make a serious mistake."

Dad thought about it for a moment, then grabbed his hat from the hook and shoved it on his head. He pulled his shotgun from the shelf above the door and the box of bullets from the drawer under the lamp. I reached for my hat, but he shook his head. "I'm going, you're not."

"But Dad-"

He shook his head. "No. I won't budge on this. If I can't stop them, I don't want you to see what happens. It might be this is just a stray wolf, but if it's not, things could get complicated pretty fast."

I tried to protest, but he pulled the door shut behind him with a bang. Mom came from the living room, the expression on her face indicating she had heard our conversation. She put a hand on my shoulder, her eyes on Dad as he climbed into the car and drove away. "He worries about you," she said gently. "He doesn't want you to get hurt."

"I'm worried about him," I replied honestly. "If this is someone like me, he could be strong enough to take out all of the hunters coming after him."

She nodded, her eyes bright with concern. "You father will be careful. It's good he's going with them."

"I should be going, too," I replied tightly.

She didn't answer and we both watched until the dust from the car faded into the evening air.

HUNTER

Chapter 4

The faint sound of gunshots met my ears long after the sun had set. I climbed out my bedroom window and swung down from the old oak tree that scratched at the glass when the wind blew. I stalked through the trees behind our house, knowing it would be foolish to try to find the hunters and make sure they were alright, but unable to sit still any longer. I paced down to the river, then followed it to where Parker's land met ours. I was about to turn back when a small sound caught my attention.

I turned my head slightly and held my breath, listening with every bit of my sensitive hearing. A slight, muffled whine sounded again. Adrenaline surged through my body. I put a hand on the fence that separated our property and vaulted over, then ran without hesitation through the dark night. I jumped logs and ducked under windfalls to a stand of big evergreens with branches so low they formed dark tents along the ground.

I stopped and held still, staring into the evergreens as my eyes made gray shapes out of the midnight forest floor. A whine sounded followed by a slight movement to my right. My heart started to race. I crept forward on the balls of my feet, stepping softly amid the pine needles that provided a nearly soundless cover. I crouched and made out the form of a cream-colored animal curled at the base of one of the trees.

A scent touched my nose and I straightened so fast I hit my head on a branch above me. I crouched again and rubbed my skull. The form moved and a head turned in my direction. My heart leaped in my throat and I couldn't breathe. I stared into the golden eyes of a cream-coated wolf.

Black stripes ran up the wolf's legs and down its back in strange patterns. One of its back legs stuck out at an odd angle, and the metallic scent of blood touched my nose. I made out the dark liquid running from a wound in the middle of its thigh. The wolf whined again, its eyes on mine, then it began to change shape.

The animal's arms and legs lengthened and joints moved while its nose flattened and ears settled down its head. Its cream fur disappeared and soft pale skin replaced it. The skin was still striped in black, and when the cream of the wolf's fur on its head changed into short, pink hair, I stared, my heart in my throat.

"Gem?" I forced out.

Pain-filled blue eyes met mine. "I'm so tired of people trying to hurt me," she said in a voice so small and tired it freed my frozen limbs.

I shrugged out of my shirt and climbed under the tree. I wrapped it around her the best I could, trying not to notice how vulnerable she was in my arms. "Aren't you afraid of me?" I asked, my voice soft.

She shook her head, her eyes closing. "You wouldn't hurt me," she said softly.

The trust in her voice sent warmth through my limbs as I held her close, trying to keep pressure on the bleeding wound in her leg. "Why is that?" I whispered.

"Because you're a werewolf, too," she replied so quietly it sounded like a sigh.

I stared down at her still form for a moment, then reality hit me that I had a naked, wounded girl in my arms, a band of angry, armed farmers looking for her, and who knew how much time to get the bullet out so she could heal properly.

"Hold on, Gem," I said, carrying her from underneath the tree. Her name tasted delicate on my tongue, like a snowflake that melts right after it lands, unique and beautiful, yet so fragile it disappears almost before it is noticed.

HUNTER

I ran faster than I had ever run before. Gem's head cradled against my bare chest, her breath a hot contrast to the chill night air. Her hand rested softly against my heart and I prayed that its strength would fill her and help her make it to safety.

I vaulted the fence between the fields without slowing. Twigs snapped to my left. I darted to the right and ducked under several sweeping branches, then jumped the massive roots of a lightning struck tree. Voices called to each other around us. I veered away from them and pushed myself faster until I reached the aspens around our property. I burst into our backyard and ran straight for the screen door. Shoving Jo barking and yipping out into the backyard with my foot, I hurried to the guest bedroom to the right of the kitchen.

"Mom! Mom, hurry!" I yelled, my heart pounding.

I settled Gem carefully on the bed and wrapped her as modestly as I could in the blankets while still leaving her bleeding leg exposed. It had bled through my shirt, but seemed to have stopped for the most part.

Mom hurried through the door. "Dray, what's wrong?" Her hand rose to her mouth and her face washed pale. "Is that a gunshot wound?" When I nodded, her eyes widened at the implications.

"Mom, we need to hurry," I urged gently.

She blinked, then nodded. "I, uh... Yes, of course. Keep pressure on it." She hurried to the kitchen and I carefully pressed on the wound. When she returned, she had hot water, rags, a sharp, small knife, a needle and thread, gauze, antiseptic, and bandages all set out on a tray.

"Have you done this before?" I asked, amazed.

She gave a small, tight smile. "I've lived on a farm all my life. Minor surgery comes with the job."

I stared at her, but she wasn't kidding. She cut my shirt

from the wound, then examined it closely. "It's healing already." She looked up at me, her eyes bright with excitement, fear, or both. "She really is like you, isn't she?"

I nodded, but she was already using the knife to enlarge the wound so she could get at the bullet. She made little swipes that didn't bleed as much as I thought they should, then pulled at the edges of the skin so she could see deeper.

Gem gave a faint moan and tried to move away from Mom's ministrations. "Hold her still, Dray. If she moves, I may cut too deep."

I whispered an apology to Gem before I held her gently but firmly, keeping her body motionless. She tensed at my touch, then her muscles eased and she relaxed as if she knew me. I studied the stripes across her skin, black marks varying from thin to thick and marking her body from her neck down to her feet. The marks beneath my touch felt like normal skin but harder and thicker, like scars. I wondered what had made them, and reasoned that it probably wasn't a good thing.

"There," Mom breathed softly. I looked over to see her drop a bullet slug onto the tray. Blood pooled out of the wound, but Mom didn't seem alarmed. She closed it with small stitches and took extra care when she tied it off. She put rubbing alcohol on some gauze and used it to clean the area around the wound, then applied antiseptic and covered it in bandages. She then wrapped Gem's leg in more gauze to hold the bandages in place.

Mom carried everything back to the kitchen and appeared a few seconds later with a nightgown. "If you'll excuse us," she said with a smile.

My cheeks turned red. It was the first time since I saw Gem change from a wolf to a girl that I consciously realized she was naked. I had been so concerned about the hunters and her safety I had forgotten everything else. Mom's look said she guessed as much and she gave me a fond pat on the cheek when I walked out of the room.

Dad found me pacing the living room. At one look at my face, he stopped putting his bullets back in the box. "What happened?"

I pointed to the guest bedroom and paused, unsure how to phrase it. "I found a wolf who was shot and brought her home. She's a new girl from school."

Dad stared. "You mean she's a werewolf?"

My soul cringed at the word we always avoided, but I nodded.

He ran a hand across his eyes and glanced toward the bedroom as if unsure whether or not he should go in there.

"Mom's putting Gem in a nightgown. She removed a bullet from her leg."

He nodded as though this didn't surprise him. "The farmers shot at a wolf they saw in the woods near Stan's place, but it lost them through the trees; they were still searching when I got there." He glanced toward the bedroom again. "I just didn't think it would really be a werewolf."

Mom came down the hall. "She's sleeping," she told us both. "She's going to be alright, but we should call her parents."

"Her last name's Hawthorne, but they just moved in so I don't know how we'll find them," I said, wanting more than anything to go in and check on her, but knowing she would probably sleep better away from strangers.

"I'll call Peggy."

Mom knew everyone in town, which was especially helpful when one of them happened to be the school secretary. Mom went to the phone in the kitchen and Dad settled in his chair by the stove. He picked up the newspaper, then glanced at the cover story and tossed it in the stove. He grabbed a magazine about a new line of tractors and began to read.

After a minute, he glanced over the top of the magazine. "You should probably go check on her. Ma's liable to be a bit."

I walked slowly down the hall feeling uncertain now that she was safe and healing. I opened the door a crack and saw that her eyes were open. She looked small and forlorn under Mom's big quilt. I pushed the door open a bit more. "Is it alright if I come in?" I asked quietly.

"Dray?" she said hesitantly. When I nodded, a soft smile spread across her face. "Thank goodness."

I took that as an invitation and stepped into the room. She tried to sit up, but then she winced and tears filled her eyes.

"Are you alright?" I hurried to her side. "Can I get you anything?"

She shook her head and turned her face into the pillow.

"Does it hurt?" I pressed, concerned.

She nodded and whispered quietly, "Can you hold me?"

I hesitated, caught off guard. I had never held hands with a girl, let alone actually comforted one; but I couldn't turn away from her quiet plea. I crawled onto the other side of the bed and sat near the pillows. She backed into my arms so that she faced away from me. I wrapped my arms around her and held her, my heart pounding so loud I wondered if she heard it.

Her breathing slowed and I thought she had fallen asleep when she said quietly, "Being held reminds me that I'm not in a cage anymore."

I frowned into her hair. "When were you in a cage?" My heart clenched at the thought.

A shiver ran through her and I held her closer. "I was

there for a long time." She fell silent again, then said, "It's hard to remember sometimes that I'm free, especially when I'm hurt."

She quieted again; after several minutes she sighed and then her breathing evened out. I held still, afraid that any movement I made would wake her up; I felt grateful she was able to escape the pain through sleep. I thought of Scotty and Preston, and smiled at what Scotty would say if he saw me. My smile fell at what my friends didn't know.

I lost track of time while I held Gem. Eventually, I decided I needed to get up in case her parents arrived. They probably wouldn't appreciate their daughter sleeping next to an unknown boy no matter how innocent it was. I eased my arm slowly out from under her shoulders and was about to climb off the bed when she screamed.

Icy adrenaline raced through my veins and I fought back an intense shudder as my body tried to change form so I could defend her. I searched the darkness for whatever had frightened her; finding nothing, I willed my heartbeat to slow. "Gem?" I asked gently.

She glanced back and recognition swept across her face. She sat up and buried her face against my chest; when I put my arms around her, I found that she was shaking like a leaf. "It's okay," I whispered. "You're safe. I'll take care of you."

Footsteps hurried down the hall and Mom opened the door. She didn't look at all surprised to see me comforting Gem. The worry in her eyes softened and she nodded. She left the door open a crack so I would hear the Hawthornes' knock.

I settled down next to Gem and she rested more comfortably on my shoulder and closed her eyes. I fought back the urge to brush a stray strand of pink hair from her cheek. I had never been so close to a girl, let alone one hurt and helpless and looking to me for comfort. I held completely still, afraid of hurting her, and afraid of doing anything remotely like crossing boundaries that were definitely blurred at the moment.

Eventually a car pulled up outside. I listened to two sets of hurried steps rush up to the house. They knocked on the front door and Mom and Dad rose. Their steps were a bit slower. For a second I worried that there were hunters at the door instead of Gem's parents, but soft, anxious voices spoke after Mom opened the door and she welcomed them inside.

"Can we see her?" a woman asked, her voice tight with concern.

"Of course," Mom replied warmly. She led the way down the hall.

I eased my arm carefully from behind Gem's head and crawled silently off the bed. I sat on a chair in the corner of the room and toyed with Mom's crocheted pillow, suddenly nervous but unable to explain why.

The door opened to reveal a petite woman with Gem's blue eyes and slender build. The man who followed towered above her; he was also skinny with brown hair and glasses. Both looked so relieved at seeing their daughter in the bed that tears showed on their cheeks. Gem's mom took her father's hand in a gesture so tender and full of relief my tension at seeing them eased.

A familiar scent touched my nose, one I recognized from Gem. I realized what it meant. "You're werewolves?"

Both of them looked at me as if just noticing me there. The husband moved protectively in front of his wife, but she stopped him with a hand on his arm and a smile on her lips. "You're the boy that saved Gem."

"And also a werewolf," her dad said, studying me.

I held perfectly still, unsure what reaction the situation

called for. My instincts urged me to change to a wolf to protect Gem and my parents from the unknown werewolves while my mind said that they were two ordinary people grateful to find their daughter safe, that they posed no threat and were loving parents who would take care of her. My heart settled somewhere in the middle.

I rose from the chair, careful to keep my tone level. "Why was she out in the woods?"

Gem's dad bristled, but his wife silenced him with another touch. "He has a right to ask," she said, her tone gentle. "He saved her from them."

He calmed and glanced at the floor. "Sorry," he said. "There's a long story behind my reactions. Why don't you come into the living room and we can talk?"

I looked back at Gem, reluctant to leave her. "She had a nightmare," I said, worried she might be scared if she awoke in a strange house with no one to comfort her.

"She always does," her father replied, his eyebrows pulled together. "That's part of the story."

Gem's mother smoothed the blankets over her. "Don't worry, dear, we'll keep the door open in case she needs us."

I gave her a grateful smile and followed them down the hall. I felt strange, like a piece of me remained behind pillowing Gem's head on my shoulder and keeping her nightmares at bay.

Chapter 5

"Gem was kidnapped seven months ago," Greg began. He sighed and stretched out his long legs. Mom and Dad sat close together on the couch and I took Mom's wooden rocking chair. I fought down a wave of nausea at the thought of Gem going through such a thing. He continued, "We searched everywhere and couldn't find her. We never gave up, even though the authorities and the werewolves we contacted to help us find her said we were beyond the threshold for getting her back. We never stopped looking, but it became harder to hope. Then we got a call a month ago."

"Five weeks," Anna corrected in the pained tones of one who counted every day they were apart.

Greg nodded. "She's right," he said with a smile. "She always is."

"Tell them who called us," Anna pressed. There was a note of awe in her voice.

"Jaze Carso was the one who called," Greg said.

The amazement in his tone caught my attention. "Who?"

Greg and Anna exchanged an incredulous look. "You don't know who Jaze Carso is?" Greg asked, looking from me to Mom and Dad.

We shook our heads and they exchanged another look. Anna's expression softened. "He's a good one to know. I guess we shouldn't be surprised you haven't heard of him out here. I just assumed everyone knew about Jaze."

Greg took her hand in his. "Jaze Carso and his team freed Gem along with about fifty other werewolves from cells that were essentially werewolf torture chambers." He took off his glasses and rubbed his eyes with the heel of his hand, then put them back on.

"We thought she was dead," he continued in a strained

voice, staring at my parents but seeing something else. "Knowing she was safe was like being given your life back." He looked at me. "You don't live when your children are in danger. Your every thought goes to them; every horrible thing that could be happening flashes through your mind. Knowing she was alright was like being able to breathe again, to think again. We drove right to the airport and demanded the first flight. Holding her in our arms. . . ." His words choked off.

Mom excused herself, then came back a few minutes later with cups of hot cocoa. Greg thanked her and took a sip, then gestured vaguely toward the door. "We moved here so that Gem could start fresh. There weren't any other werewolves as far as we knew," he glanced at me again and gave a small shrug, "But when Gem said she made friends with one at school, she seemed so happy about it we didn't mind."

The thought that she counted me a friend made my soul lighter, but my chest tightened when he continued, "She's had nightmares every night since she was kidnapped. The marks on her body are from whips with silver in them. They still hurt her even though they've healed. She likes to run at night because it wears her out and helps her sleep better." He sighed. "I didn't know the farmers were going after wolves. I'm just glad they didn't know to use silver bullets."

"So werewolves are allergic to silver," Dad said. At Greg's questioning look, he explained, "We adopted Dray when he was two years old. He's the only werewolf around here. We didn't know anything about them until he changed when he was seven."

"Phased," Greg said with an understanding smile. "Changing from wolf to human or human to wolf is called phasing."

Mom's face lit up and she sat forward on the sofa. "Is there a way to keep a," she paused, the word still hard for her to get used to, "Werewolf, from phasing at the full moon?"

Greg shook his head. "We don't have a choice. All werewolves give heed to the call of the moon." He met my eyes. "But it's not necessarily a bad thing, just something that requires caution and the proper place to phase. Running with a pack is nice because you have safety in numbers and can watch out for each other."

A question came to my mind. "Are you the werewolves who have been killing cows and sheep around here?"

Greg looked insulted. "We would never kill farm animals."

"Sorry," I apologized quickly. "I didn't mean any offense. I just didn't know because they started the same time you got here."

He frowned. "I understand, but it wasn't us. It sounds like it was several werewolves." He looked at me seriously. "You may have a new pack trying to move in on your territory."

The thought sent a chill down my spine; where before the idea of other werewolves was a welcome one, the thought of a pack who killed livestock so close to town unnerved me.

"What do we do?" I asked.

He glanced at Mom and Dad. "You can either wait for them to surface, or hunt them out, but if they're making trouble, Jaze has several groups prepared to deal with such things."

Gem's parents slept in my room and I bunked on the living room floor in front of the stove. I awoke at every sound from the guest room, but Gem's mom, Anna, was at the door before I even got to my feet. She gave me a grateful smile just before sunrise.

"It's nice to know there's another light sleeper here."

"I worry about her," I said.

She nodded. "I do, too. But I'm thankful she's found a friend."

"Me, too," I whispered when she closed the door to my room.

***

The next morning after the cows had been fed and milked, we sat at the kitchen table eating fresh pancakes with marmalade and grapefruit juice when the door to the guest bedroom opened. Anna and Greg rose and I stood with them when Gem limped into the room, her pink hair disheveled and face pale, but the smile I was quickly growing to love on her face.

"Good morning," she said with a shy cast to her eyes.

Anna gave her a tight hug. "How are you feeling, darling?"

"Much better," Gem replied. She met my eyes over her mom's shoulder. "Thank you," she mouthed, a shadow of pain in her gaze.

"Anytime," I mouthed in reply.

Greg gave his daughter a hug next and pulled out a chair for her. She sat gingerly and smiled at Mom and Dad. "You're so kind to open your home to us."

"You're welcome here anytime," Mom said warmly.

Dad scooted the plate of pancakes over to her. "If there's anything I've learned about living with a werewolf, it's that they can eat."

Everyone looked at the huge stack of pancakes on my plate and started to laugh. I rolled my eyes, but Gem grinned and I laughed, too.

"So what are you plans in Thistle?" Dad asked.

Greg poured syrup over his pancakes. "We moved here to start over as a family and put the past behind us." He looked at Gem, but she toyed with her fork in a small puddle of syrup on her plate. Greg smiled anyway. "I think Thistle will be a great place for all of us to find new lives."

HUNTER

***

Gem met me on Monday and we walked to school together. My thoughts had been on the werewolf pack all weekend, at least when my thoughts weren't on Gem. I wanted to track them down, but Gem thought it was a bad idea.

"It's the only way to protect our town," I argued.

Gem shook her head, her pink hair bright against the light of the rising sun behind us. "What if they're hostile?"

"Then they shouldn't be here and need to be encouraged to move on."

"By one werewolf?" Her eyebrows rose. "You really think they'll listen?"

I gritted my teeth. "They will if they know what's good for them. You don't mess with someone's livelihood. The two bulls they killed last night were worth a fortune. Daniel's raised them since they were calves and showed them at the Fair. He could lead them around like puppies."

She skipped lightly in front of me. I was amazed at how quickly she had healed given the state she was in when I found her. I had expected her to stay home from school, but she showed up at my house saying she had missed enough already and skipping a Monday threw off the entire week. When I asked what her parents thought, she said they would survive it.

"They keep me on such a tight leash. I know they're just getting over me being gone, but I need my space." She plucked a long blade of wheat and dusted it along the road. "Sometimes it's easier to be alone than to feel them watching me all the time worried I'll disappear."

She glanced at me suddenly as if the admission was by accident. I nodded, glad she was comfortable with opening up a tiny bit. "I understand at least a little. When my parents realized I was. . . different, they worried someone would find out. Luckily we don't have too many visitors on the farm. I didn't have to be careful until school."

"It's strange to be in a place without werewolves, and a little bit nice," Gem admitted. Her face colored as if she realized what she had said. "Not that I mind being around you," she rushed on. "I just like not having to worry about hierarchy or Alphas. It's nice not being told what to do."

I stared at her. "Alphas tell you what to do?"

She opened her mouth to give a quick answer, then thought about it for a moment and shrugged. "I guess not that much. But if they tell you to do something, you have to listen."

"Why?"

She gave me a serious look. "Because they're in charge. Order is very important in a pack. It creates harmony and balance."

"But you hate it?" I pressed.

She gave a short, musical laugh. "I hate it. I hate anything that has to do with order. No one should be able to control anyone else's life." She stopped with her mouth open, then gave me a sideways glance. "I don't know about you, Dray Dawson."

"What about me?" I asked.

Her eyes creased at the corners. "You have a peculiar way of getting me to say things I don't mean to."

I gave her my most winning smile. "Don't you trust me?"

She laughed again. "I'm not so sure you want to hear the depths of my soul."

"Somehow I don't believe they're as dark and horrible as you think they are," I replied.

She gave me another look, this time one more thoughtful and penetrating. "I should probably hang around you more.

It might be good for me."

"I know of a good werewolf hunting activity," I hinted.

She gave in. "I'll go with you, but I think you might be biting off more than you can chew." She laughed, a light, bright sound that reminded me of Christmas bells or little birds flitting about.

"Thanks," I mumbled, sure she was making fun of me.

She laughed again and grabbed my arm. "Smile, dreary Dray. Life is amazing. There's so much worth being happy about, and somehow being around you reminds me of that."

I glanced at her and couldn't help it. Her eyes were so brilliantly blue they looked like a still pond reflecting the blue sky a hundred times over; the way she looked at me made my heart skip sideways in my chest, something I wasn't exactly sure was healthy, but that filled me with strength and energy. She practically floated over the sidewalk, her skipping feet barely touching the ground. It felt like her grip on my arm was the only thing keeping her down.

I smiled and she nodded in acceptance of it. She tried to take her backpack back, but I refused to give it to her which made her smile even more.

"I just wish I knew where to start," I mused out loud.

She glanced at me and her eyes danced as though she held in a secret.

"What?"

She shrugged. "It is my duty to point out that you have entirely missed the benefits of being a werewolf."

"And they are?" I questioned doubtfully.

"Acute hearing, great night vision, and," she paused dramatically, "A highly developed sense of smell."

I swept a hand through my hair to push it off my forehead and glanced at her. "Are you saying we should track them like a coon hound?"

She nodded, her white teeth showing, "Or track them like wolves, since wolves were the first to do it."

I eyed her curiously. "Where are we going to get their scent?"

"From the bulls, or the sheep, or cows, or the Crastons' chickens they got the other night." She grimaced. "Although I don't know why they bothered. Cleaned chicken is fine, but all those feathers and bones? It's a waste of time."

I stared at her and she gave me a reproachful look. "Not everyone has the spotless past you do. I'd be lying if I said I didn't get into trouble once in a while back home, but Mom and Dad never got mad." Her voice tightened. "They were always there for me."

I glanced at her. She had stopped skipping and walked almost normally beside me. She held her arms across her chest and rubbed them self-consciously despite her long sleeved shirt.

"Track them it is," I said to take her back to a lighter subject. "First thing after school."

She smiled. "Deal."

Chapter 6

Coach Matthews pulled me aside during gym again and asked if I had enjoyed the game. I told him honestly that I had and he just smiled and left it at that. I jogged my laps behind Preston and Scotty. Preston tried to trip Scotty, then ended up tripping himself. I had to jump over him to avoid falling, and when I glanced up, the Coach gave me a thumbs-up. I sighed and helped Preston back to his feet and we ran to catch up to Scotty.

"He's really pushing you," Scotty mentioned after class.

"He knows winter's coming and farm work slows down," Preston echoed. "You're going to run out of excuses."

"I don't know why you just don't do it," Scotty said. He slung his backpack over his shoulder as we left the gymnasium and walked down the sidewalk to school.

"Football's just not my thing," I said, though my tone was unconvincing.

Scotty rolled his eyes. "I've seen you throw a ball. Nobody throws like that unless they've really practiced." He put a hand on my shoulder, making me stop. "What's the real reason you don't want to play?"

Preston looked from Scotty to me expectantly. I wanted to tell them and had tried on several different occasions, but letting someone know you turn into a wolf at the full moon wasn't exactly an easy topic to approach.

I eventually gave up and avoided it, but it left a few moments that needed explaining, like the time Tom and Jorge were driving drunk and hit Preston's car. Preston and Scotty were beat up pretty bad in the accident, but I was barely scratched. I had to take a short walk to avoid phasing and giving in to the urge to tear Tom and Jorge apart. There was the night we went to Olivia's party and I forgot about the full moon until Mom called me in a panic and I ran home instead of waiting to be picked up. There was also the time the junkyard Rottweiler chased us until I turned and growled at it, then it ran away yelping like a scolded puppy.

I felt like I was protecting them by hiding my secret. I didn't know enough about it to explain it, and I didn't want them to be accomplices if I was ever found out.

We walked through the back doors of the school with the other students returning from the gym. I studied the yellowing floor tiles, wondering what kind of an excuse would get me out of the football questions. I was saved the trouble when Gem came running up, her face flushed and blue eyes sparkling. She slowed when she realized I was with friends and stopped a few feet away.

I smiled at her. "Preston, Scotty, this is Gem."

Preston's eyes widened and he grinned, his cheeks turning as red as his hair. "Nice to meet you. I'm the mascot. I mean, I'm not really the mascot, but I play the mascot." He frowned. "I mean I don't play the mascot, I wear the mascot costume for football and basketball games. I'm a giant ear of corn."

Gem smiled. "Any ear of corn that's a friend of Dray's is a friend of mine."

Preston laughed so hard he snorted, then covered his mouth with both hands in embarrassment.

Scotty merely nodded. "We've met."

Gem's eyes darkened slightly and she tipped her head to the side. "You're the one who gave me a cheesy pickup line and asked if I would like to be your girlfriend even though you knew nothing about me."

"Can't blame a guy for trying," Scotty replied under his breath.

Gem gave him a soothing smile. "You were charming,

but I was being honest. I really have too much studying to do to give any guy attention."

"Except Dray?" Scotty said directly, putting me on the spot.

Gem glanced at me and I could see her thinking quickly. She smiled. "Well, he's friend of the family."

Scotty's eyes narrowed and he looked at me; there was a brief glimmer of hope in his eyes at salvaging his wounded pride. "She's right," I admitted, throwing her a quick glance. "I didn't know it when I first saw Gem, but our parents are good friends."

"From college," she shot in.

I grinned and Gem fell in beside us. We joined the throng of students at the lunchroom and waited for chicken fingers, a garden salad, and canned pears. Gem picked chocolate milk while I went with regular. She lifted her eyebrows. "Enjoy life," she whispered with sincere undertones. "You never know when you might miss chocolate milk."

I gave in and exchanged my milk for a chocolate one, then paid for both of our lunches. Gem tried to argue, but at a dollar and a half, it was the cheapest lunch I would probably ever buy for a girl.

"Big spender?" Scotty teased, but his frustration was gone and it felt good to see his confident side again. "You really should get him to take you somewhere nice," he said in a loud voice to Gem.

"I will," she agreed. "Then he'll wish he'd let me pay."

Scotty laughed and followed us to our usual table. Gem sat down and gave me a searching look. Preston was still in line to pay, so she asked Scotty to get her some ketchup. "Who eats chicken with ketchup?" he argued, but he was flattered by the request and went to get her some.

She leaned across the table toward me. "They got

someone else's cows."

It took me a minute to realize she was talking about the werewolves. "Do you know who's they were?"

"The Wilsons," she replied and I fought back the urge to growl. According the Dad, it was Jeff Wilson who shot Gem. She lifted an eyebrow at the look on my face and I took a calming breath. "Alright, at least we know where the trail is freshest."

She grinned. "Now you're starting to sound like a werewolf."

I stared at her, amazed that she would say the word aloud in a lunchroom full of students. She nonchalantly ate a chicken finger as Scotty came back with the ketchup.

HUNTER

***

"You shouldn't be ashamed of what you are."

"Well you shouldn't go blabbing it all over school," I replied, studying the bloodstained ground. My stomach turned over at the dried entrails and flesh the Wilsons had left when they took the bodies away.

"It's not like anyone heard me," Gem replied, nudging a lone hoof with her toe.

"They might have."

She looked up at my tone. "Dray, you're a werewolf. You'll be a lot happier when you've accepted the fact and stop worrying about what humans think."

I said the words I had told myself over and over again since the first time I phased. "I am human."

Gem opened her mouth to say something, but she must have seen the desperation on my face because she closed it again and nodded. We wandered around the kill site for several more minutes in silence. I finally swallowed the knot in my throat and said, "I'm sorry, Gem. This is a lot for me. I've just got to get used to it."

She smiled in acceptance. "Ten years hasn't been enough?"

I rolled my eyes and gestured to the mess. "Where do we start?"

She studied the ground thoughtfully, then walked to the edge of the Wilson's back forty. "They left through here."

"How can you tell?" The grass on the other side of the fence looked like the long grass for five miles around.

She crouched and pointed to dark red marks on a few blades of grass. I noticed that several were bent. "Smell," she said softly.

I sniffed and a million scents tangled in my nose, the sun-worn wood of the fence we leaned on, the ants that scurried up and down the poles with bits of grass and leaves in their mouths, the cow pies behind us, dried and smelling of partially-digested grass, the decaying leftovers from the werewolves' meal a few paces away, and the sunshine and strawberry scent of the girl crouched next to me, her nimble fingers braiding several strands of grass and her breath brushing my face with the smell of ketchup, chicken fingers, and the peppermint gum she chewed.

I shook my head. "I can't find it; there are too many other scents."

She stood and walked behind me, then soft fingers covered my eyes. "Smell," she whispered in my ear.

It took every ounce of self-control I had not to turn around and kiss her.

The thought surprised me. I had never felt like that about a girl. I had butterflies in my stomach and my heart felt like it skipped every-other beat. I took several deep breaths to remind myself of why we were here and to rationalize that I didn't want our first kiss to be in the middle of a cow pasture next to the entrails of several slaughtered Holsteins; the thought that I wanted a first kiss distracted me above anything.

"Can you smell it?" she asked, her breath tickling my ear.

I pushed the chaotic thoughts away and concentrated. I took a deep breath, then another. The scents from before crowded together, then fell away to reveal the musky werewolf scent that matched Gem and her parents. The scent parted to form at least seven individual scents, all with the werewolf undertones. "I smell it," I said, the awe I felt touching my voice.

She dropped her hands and skipped around me. "Amazing, isn't it?"

I nodded. "It's like someone handed me a picture, but

instead of using paint, they used scents."

Her nose wrinkled. "Not the best analogy, but I'll take it." She jumped over the fence and asked eagerly, "What are you waiting for?"

She looked so petite and cute with her hands on her hips and her head tipped to one side like a puppy that I wished I had a camera so I could keep the image forever. I committed it to memory and laughed when she went dancing along the trail like a graceful, caffeine-addled butterfly. "Wait up," I called. "I can't follow the trail that fast."

"Then leave it to me," she said over her shoulder. "I'll be your coon hound."

I laughed and ran to catch up to her.

***

A prickling sensation ran down my spine again. "Do you feel that?"

Gem shook her head but her voice was soft, her attention on the trees. "What?"

I peered through the scattered trees of the national forest below town. "It feels like we're being watched." We had followed the trail far out of town to the tree line. Gem didn't want to go in, but I couldn't give up, not with the town's livestock at risk. The scent of werewolf was everywhere. I hadn't used my nose for tracking often enough to tell if the scents were fresh, but they were strong.

A twig snapped and I stepped in front of Gem. My heart slowed when six werewolves came out from behind trees, boulders, and a windfall. Pine needles broke softy behind us and I glanced back to see two more werewolves. The two behind us smelled feral and unwashed, but the wind blew at our backs so I couldn't smell those in front. I made a mental note to keep that in mind next time I tracked a pack of potentially dangerous werewolves.

The six in front of us wore scattered bits of clothing or rags tied with ropes and string. They had mostly bare feet, dirty arms and legs, and a wild look in their eyes. I hadn't considered the possibility that werewolves could be wild.

In my naive mind, I had pictured us having a civilized talk with an Alpha or whoever led the pack to our town, him seeing the error of his ways and agreeing to take his pack somewhere else so they wouldn't be eating livestock, and everyone shaking hands and going their separate directions.

The way these werewolves looked at us let me know I had made a very big mistake.

"You following us?" a man with matted brown hair and scratches across his face asked. His eyes were narrow and his expression vicious.

"We're just out walking," I explained quickly, hoping Gem would go along with my story. "We'd better be getting back now."

The first man shook his head. "You're lying." He nodded back the way we had come. "We saw you pick up our trail and follow it here. You've come to chase us out." He took a deep breath of our scent flowing to him on the evening breeze. "You're protecting your little home."

He took a step closer and my muscles tightened. The predatory way he looked at Gem sent a rush of anger through my limbs.

"Your presence here is seriously lacking in good judgment. We're not leaving," he growled, his gaze burning into mine. He clenched his fists and the sinews in his arms and hands stood out sharply from his lean frame. "So you'd better let us be."

I wanted to fight him. Everything about his stance and his gaze begged me to attack, to give him a reason to fight. I wanted to meet his challenge so fiercely that the blood burned in my veins, but a quiet breath beside me made me pause.

"Let's go," Gem whispered so softly I almost didn't hear it. "Drop your eyes and turn around. It's the only way we're getting out of this."

I didn't have any fighting experience and would certainly go down under an attack of eight werewolves, two of whom I was surprised to realize were female, but who looked just as angry, volatile, and feral as the one who spoke. If I went down, Gem would be left defenseless.

Pride and instinct bade me to fight and defend my territory, but my brain told me I couldn't beat the odds. If I let pride win, Gem would pay for my foolishness. I dropped my eyes and turned away. Gem and I walked in short, measured steps past the two werewolves who waited behind us. We didn't speak or go faster for the next several miles. Tremors ran up my spine at the feeling of the werewolves at our heels, but I didn't turn around.

We had almost reached the fence at the Wilsons when the feeling eased, then vanished. I helped Gem over the fence, then followed slowly behind her.

"I can't believe we were so stupid," Gem said when we reached my truck parked near the stop sign across from the Wilsons' north field.

"They would have killed us, wouldn't they?" I asked, though I already knew the answer by the look in their eyes.

She nodded. "But there's no Alpha."

I glanced at her, surprised. "How could you tell?"

"The way they held themselves, the way they met our eyes and looked away. I don't know, but it's a feeling. You'll know the first time you meet an Alpha," she said. "They're in charge and they know it. I don't know how else to explain it."

I opened her door, then walked around the truck and climbed into the driver's seat. "What does it mean if there are eight werewolves in a pack without an Alpha?"

She looked worried. "I don't know, but it's unusual. I'll have to call Vance and see what he thinks."

I glanced at her as I drove up to the stop sign. "Who's Vance?" I tried to ignore the jealousy I felt at her talking about another guy.

She fell silent for a minute, then took a breath and gave a brittle smile. "A werewolf I met at Lobotraz where we were tortured. He's the one who got me out."

Guilt chased away the jealousy. "Then I'd like to tell him thank you," I replied sincerely.

Her smile turned bright and strong like sunbeams

streaming through a path of clouds. She set a hand on my arm and kept it there.

We drove down Thistle's main street and were stopped at the one streetlight in town when the doors to the firehouse at the corner lifted and both of the town's fire engines roared to life. Their sirens pierced the air and I had to fight the urge to cover my ears. Gem covered hers and winced at the sound.

It echoed around us as if caught in the truck. I wanted to put some distance between us and the sirens, but something kept my attention. On impulse, I followed the engines when the light turned green.

"Where are you going?" Gem shouted with her ears still covered.

"I'm not sure," I yelled back. We turned onto Third Street and my heart skipped a beat. The hospital was on fire.

Thistle had a new two-story, fifty-room hospital with a helipad on top. It was bigger than the town needed, but we catered to a lot of the smaller towns scattered along the freeway. The white walls, gray tinted windows, and the state of the art emergency room were the pride of the town; now smoke tangled from broken windows on the second floor.

The fire engines pulled up to the front with their lights flashing and sirens still wailing. I gunned the old truck and it shuddered in protest as we raced down the road and skidded in the gravel across the street from the hospital. I jumped out with Gem close behind me.

Roughly twenty patients sat or stood on the lawn of the library next to the hospital. Nurses and doctors tended to them while others brought blankets from nearby houses. Several patients looked like they suffered from smoke inhalation; medical teams gave them oxygen from the ambulances and tended to minor injuries.

I recognized Dr. Caroe in the fray; we delivered hay to

him each winter to feed his prized Arabian stallion. I grabbed his arm. "What happened?"

His eyes looked past me to the patients on the lawn. "A fire started in the stairwell and it spread faster than anything I've ever seen." He motioned toward the patients. "I've got to go."

I let him pass, then ran around to the back of the hospital.

"Dray, where are you going?" Gem demanded, following me.

I opened the door, then stepped back when smoke billowed out. "What's the use of being stronger than anyone else if you don't use it?" I asked. Faint cries for help and the hungry snap and hiss of flames snaked through the door. I ducked inside before she could come up with a reply.

I had never been to the hospital for myself, but we use to visit Mom's aunt when she was bedridden. I pictured the floor layout and turned left, thinking to use the back stairs if the front were out of commission from the fire. When I reached the corner, angry flames spiraled across the ceiling, eating at the ceiling tiles and sending out blankets of heat that made me duck back behind the wall for protection.

Something in the middle of the main floor caught my eye and I froze in disbelief.

"We've got to hurry," Gem said. She grabbed my arm, but I didn't move. She followed my gaze, then gasped. "Is that what I think it is?"

I took a step closer, but it was obviously a bull's hoof with dried blood crusted around the bone. I gritted my teeth. "How is that possible?" I demanded. "We just left them!"

Gem shook her head. "We'll figure it out later. There's not time right now. Follow me." She hurried along the wall to the elevator and tried to pull at the doors. When they didn't budge, she called for me to help her. I picked up a chair and wedged the leg in the door, then used it to pry them halfway open. Gem stepped inside without hesitation.

"What are you doing?" I demanded.

"Give me a leg up," she insisted, pointing to the escape hatch on top.

I lifted her and she pushed the hatch open, then pulled herself up. "Come on," she shouted.

I jumped and grabbed the edge of the elevator roof, then pulled myself up after her. Gem was already climbing the cables toward the next floor. I told myself she was crazy as I climbed up after her. We reached the second floor and pushed open the doors.

Flames lapped hungrily at the oxygen from the elevator shaft and we had to duck to the sides to avoid the heat. "This is insane," Gem shouted, her eyes wide and face pale.

I nodded in agreement, but I refused to leave the hospital if there were patients who were trapped and couldn't get out. I fell to my knees, then crawled along the floor to the first room. Gem's hand grabbed my leg as she followed through the thick blanket of smoke.

The first room was empty, as was the second. We were about to leave the third when a sound caught my ear. I followed it to the bathroom and opened the door to see a little old lady in a hospital gown clutching a vase of flowers to her chest.

She coughed as smoke rushed in. "Duck down," I shouted over the angry roar of the flames. She just stared at me, her eyes watery and clouded. I grabbed her behind the knees and lifted so that she rested on my shoulder. It wasn't a very prince charming rescue type of move, but it got us back through the door and down the long hall to the window at the end.

Gem grabbed a chair from the closest room and threw it through the glass. The window shattered outward and smoke billowed with it. I set the old woman gently on the floor to the side of the window and leaned out, heedless of the glass that cut at my hands. "Help," I shouted, waving my arms.

A fire truck was lifting its ladder up to a window a few yards away, but they stopped when they saw me. I couldn't hear what they yelled above the roar of the flames, but I assumed they would be up soon. I ducked back down next to Gem and the woman.

"Stay with her," I commanded. "I need to check the other rooms." I left before Gem could argue and crawled quickly back down the hall, checking the rooms as much with my hands and nose as with sight through the thickening smoke. The scent of burning wires and caustic plastics scorched my lungs with every breath. I called out in each room, but heard no response. I told myself I would check one more, then leave. The fire that roared around me made even that decision a potentially life-threatening one.

I felt through the room and a scent touched my nose. I followed it to a young boy with a cast on both arms. He was huddled in a corner, his awkward casts leaving his arms angled in front of him.

"Are you alright?" I asked loudly.

He nodded quickly, his dark eyes bright with fear.

"Hold onto me," I told him, picking him up so that he leaned against my hip. He wrapped his arms as well as he could around my neck and I ducked back out the door.

The smoke was thick and the heat of the fire writhing along the ceiling was almost unbearable. I shielded the boy with my body the best that I could and ran down the hall.

"Dray, Dray hurry!" Gem shouted.

I was almost there when I passed a muffled cry in a room

on my right. I counted my steps to the window and fell beneath it, gasping for air.

Firemen had reached the window and were helping the old woman onto the ladder. I handed Gem the little boy. "Where are you going?" she demanded. "You can't go back in there!"

I glanced over my shoulder to see orange flames licking the sides of the hallway and smoke as black as midnight clouding everything. I took several deep breaths of the fresh air that flowed through the window. "Come out, son," one of the firemen at the window said.

I shook my head. "There's someone else. I'll be right back."

"Wait," both he and Gem called, but I was already lost in the smoke.

I ran down the middle of the hall feeling the bottom of my cowboy boots burn with the heat of the fire eating up from the floor below. I counted my steps, then reached for a door to the left. There wasn't one. I felt along the flaming wall quickly, searching for an opening. I found one and dove through the door, then began to call frantically.

There was no answer. Either I was in the wrong room or the person had passed out from the smoke. I searched the ground on my hands and knees, then remembered the old woman's room and opened the bathroom door. A form lay at the bottom. I patted quickly, found the man's head, then listened and felt for breathing. His chest rose and fell shallowly.

It took a considerable effort to get him over my shoulder. The toxic fumes were taking their toll as my lungs struggled for air. I stumbled hard against the door frame, then righted myself and pushed through into the burning hallway. I got turned around in the smoke and flames and couldn't tell if I was heading toward the window or the elevator. I stumbled forward, knowing I was either going to plummet through the open elevator shaft or out the window.

I gasped for air. My lungs burned and my smoke-filled vision narrowed to a single dot of light that flickered in the distance. I staggered toward it, no longer thinking; only the fierce survival instincts of the wolf kept one foot moving in front of the other.

I reached the light and fell through it. Arms caught me.

HUNTER

Chapter 7

"Dray?"

The nightmare played over and over again, flames, a never-ending hallway, Gem over my shoulder pleading silently with her bright blue eyes for me to rescue her, and a single dot of light that danced continually out of reach.

"Dray?"

I gasped and the nightmare faded. My lungs burned with the intake of air. The scent of paper and books touched my nose along with lingering smoke, singed hair, burned skin, and bandages and antiseptic. I opened my eyes slowly.

The lights were dim, but I could make out shelves of books stretching down each side of my makeshift bed.

"Dray?"

I turned and saw Mom looking down at me; her face showed a mixture of concern and relief. She smoothed the hair back from my forehead. "How are you feeling?"

"I-" I coughed and my lungs hurt, but though my voice croaked, the pain was already fading. "Alright," I finished, smiling at how pathetic I sounded.

"I can tell," Mom replied with a worried smile.

I pushed up slowly from the bed and even though I could tell she wanted to keep me down, Mom let me sit up. "What day is it?" My arms and legs felt weird; they were achy and sore, but also tense as though ready for something.

"Tuesday night," Mom replied. There was weight to the way she said the words that made them important.

I thought for a minute, then an icy chill ran through my body. "The full moon."

She nodded. "You've slept for almost two days." She gave a soft, motherly smile. "And you deserved it after what you did, but we need to go."

I stood slowly and she grabbed my arm to support me, but I didn't need it. The weakness from the bad air had vanished and left in its place only an urgent need to go out in the night before I phased indoors and we were all in trouble. "Are we in the library?"

Mom nodded. "They opened it to the patients. It's become a backup hospital until they get the other one rebuilt."

"How bad was it?"

"Gutted," she said, her voice heavy.

My chest tightened. "We didn't get everyone out, did we?"

She looked like she didn't want to answer, but Mom never lied to me. She shook her head, but said, "You did what you could, and you almost died there, too. Three people are still alive because of you."

Anger filled me so violently I turned and punched one of the book shelves for lack of a better outlet. The shelf rocked back and forth and several books fell to the floor before it settled. "It's the werewolves. They need to be stopped."

Mom's face washed white with shock as much at the fact that I just said werewolf in public as the fact that I blamed the fire on the werewolf pack.

An elderly woman with wild hair peered around the corner. I picked up one of the books I had knocked off and waved it in her direction. "It's 'The Hound of the Baskervilles', a very good book," I explained, trying to cover up for my outburst. "They think a werewolf's after them and it needs to be stopped."

She looked at me like I was crazy and disappeared around the corner again.

"Let's talk about it at home," Mom said quietly. She took the book from my hand and placed it back on the shelf.

"There are patients trying to rest, and we have pressing matters to attend to."

I willed my muscles to relax and let Mom lead me through the library. Dad, Gem, and Gem's parents rose from chairs in the reading corner and hurried over.

Dad looked me up and down. "How are you feeling?"

I shrugged. "Fine, except for an overwhelming need for vengeance."

Greg nodded. "Gem told us about the cow hoof. We've already called Jaze and he's trying to find out where the werewolves came from." He glanced outside and his shoulder muscles twitched. "But we're cutting things a bit close. We'd better get going."

Gem slipped her hand into mine and we walked out of the library and into the hazy gray of the smoke-washed sunset. It felt right walking next to Gem. She was the first girl who had ever wanted to hold my hand, but it didn't feel awkward or forced, it felt natural as if her fingers had been made to fit with mine. I glanced at her, wondering if she felt the same way, but she kept her eyes on the sky and the vanishing sun.

The first light of the full moon that peeked over the trees blanketed my shoulders, easing some of the anger from my chest but lacing it deep into my soul to be dealt with later. I took a breath of the night air and winced at the lingering bite of chemical smoke and the memories it brought. Gem squeezed my hand and we climbed into my truck.

Dad tapped on the window. "You sure you're fit to drive?" he asked through the glass.

I unrolled it. "I feel fine. I think I just inhaled too much smoke."

He nodded, then surprised me by squeezing my shoulder. "I'm glad you're alright."

Greg and Anna walked up behind him. "Don't worry, Jason, we'll take good care of him."

Something that looked like hint of envy swept through his eyes so quickly I might have imagined it before he thanked Gem's parents and went back to the town car with Mom. Greg drove south and I followed him slowly.

"Are you sure you're alright?" Gem asked after a couple of minutes.

I smiled at the concern in her voice. "I'm fine, really."

She reached out and touched a singed strand of my blond hair. Surprised, I tipped the rear view mirror down and stared at my soot-smudged face and the shadows under my eyes. The tips of my hair were black and curled at the ends. I wished I had my hat so I could cover it up. I adjusted the mirror back and straightened in my seat. "I guess I got lucky."

Gem intertwined her fingers together and stared out the front window. "When you didn't come back, I was so worried. I yelled and yelled, but the fireman wouldn't let me go find you. Then when you came through the smoke, your clothes were on fire and your eyes were red as you carried that man." Her voice tightened and she looked down at her hands in her lap. "Then you collapsed right in front of me and I thought you'd died."

I hadn't known any of it, and didn't even realize until she pointed it out that I was wearing different clothes. I glanced down at my feet and saw that I wore my old boots Mom hung onto for when I mowed the lawn or mucked out the cow shed. A slight odor of cow manure wafted from them and I wrinkled my nose.

"Don't worry," Gem said, mistaking my expression. "You mother's the one who changed your clothes."

I laughed, then lifted up an arm and she slid underneath it, resting comfortably against my side. My little green truck whirred faithfully after the Hawthornes' red car. I felt Gem slide closer and in a bold moment smoothed her pink pixie hair. "I'm sorry I scared you back there."

She was silent, then said, "I lost too many friends at Lobotraz. It was hard to see them leave the cages and wonder if they'll ever return." She sniffed and buried her head against my chest. "Waiting for you to come back through the smoke felt just like that, not knowing if you were dead or too hurt to move, or if you were waiting for someone to rescue you."

Guilt washed over me so strong I could barely breathe. My dreams of playing football, my worry of what my friends would think of me if they ever found out I was a werewolf, having to feed cows and work on the farm instead of participate at school events, it all felt so petty and small. Gem had been tortured and near death for six months, not knowing if she would ever get out and watching her friends vanish one by one. My heart thumped heavily and I held my arm more securely around her. "You'll never have to worry like that again. I promise I'll always come back, no matter what. I won't let anyone hurt you."

She nodded, then sat up again. She wiped her eyes and watched out the window. The rising moon lit the scattered forest so it looked like fingers reaching from the ground, trying to catch the bright orb in its embrace. The effect was hauntingly beautiful and a chill ran down my spine.

Gem glanced at me with a shadow of her usual smile. "Try to wait a few minutes longer. Phasing while driving is highly frowned upon."

I laughed and tightened my fingers on the steering wheel, reminding my body that I needed to stay human for a little bit longer. The thought made me sober. "Are we human?" I asked quietly.

Gem looked like she was going to give a flippant answer,

then she paused at the look on my face and thought for a minute. When she replied, her voice was soft and gentle. "I don't think so. Dad explains it like we're a different race, a species with hidden abilities."

I snorted. "Sounds straight out of a fantasy novel."

She gave me a serious look. "So are we, pretty much. At least, that's how humans would see us if they ever knew."

"They." It was strange to think of humans as 'they' instead of being a part of them. I wasn't sure how I felt about it.

She touched my arm. "It's not bad to be different, you know. It's alright. We can still live normal lives, and," she lifted her eyebrows, "Use our hidden abilities to help those weaker than ourselves."

"Like superheroes," I said with a smile.

She nodded, a pleased grin on her face and her blue eyes dancing. "Exactly."

She sat back, satisfied, as her parents pulled down a little side road away from the highway and I followed them through the dark trees. They turned off their headlights and I did the same. I used to drive with my headlights off all the time because with my werewolf eyesight it was easier to see without them, then I got a ticket and quit doing it. I forgot how much easier it was to see the life of the forest without bouncing lights that lit only a small section of the world outside the car.

Bathed in brilliant moonlight and faint starlight, the clearing where we finally stopped looked like the most beautiful place on earth. I climbed out of the truck in time to see two adult wolves walking through the clearing. Anna's coat was cream-colored like her daughter's, except that Gem's had black stripes in her fur where she had been whipped. Greg waited patiently behind his wife, his dark gray coat blending with the shadows of night. Gem got out on the other side of my truck and phased, then trotted around to me.

"I, uh," I stammered. I had never phased in front of anyone except Mom and Dad, and even then they had given me my privacy after I turned eight. Greg snorted in soft understanding. He turned and trotted slowly through the meadow, Anna and Gem close behind.

I waited a moment, then slowly removed my clothes and stood feeling exposed and vulnerable while I waited to phase. I worried that Gem's family would come back, or someone else would arrive at our clearing despite the fact that we were miles away from anyone. Thoughts of the fire, the werewolves, and worry over Thistle's livestock tangled through my mind until I could barely think.

I leaned against the truck and watched the moonlight splay over my hand. The brush of light felt almost tangible, like the softest flower petal or a wisp of mist over the river on hot days. Warmth flowed through my skin; I closed my eyes and let it chase away the tumultuous thoughts. Memories of moonlit runs, the scent of rabbits and wild turkeys, and endless fields and trees separated only by easily jumped fences sent a shudder through my skin.

I crouched and let the phase happen. It felt wonderful for my bones and muscles to take on the remembered shape. I had never been able to describe to Mom and Dad the warm feeling of thick fur settling over my shoulders, or how safe I felt under the embrace of the moon, like having a friend who would always watch over me.

I gave up trying to explain it when I caught them exchanging concerned glances as they tried to understand how I felt. When I was younger, I also worried that if I became too different from the little boy they had adopted they would care less about me, but as I grew up I realized that would never be the case. They loved me no matter what I became.

I rose and stretched, feeling my muscles pull and settle into place, then I shook and trotted out to where Greg, Anna, and Gem had left the meadow. I followed the bent grass to the edge of the clearing and was about to enter the trees when a creamy white muzzle poked out.

Gem's eyes appeared after, golden but still bright and teasing. She barked and then ran off after her parents. I followed along close behind. Running with a pack felt strange and complete, like something had been repaired in my soul. It was amazing to be with others like myself instead of a stranger in my own body, not sure where I belonged.

Gem moved as a wolf like she did when she was in her human form, light and fleeting, dancing from here to there on paws that merely brushed the ground before springing away. She jumped and skipped, snapping at stray leaves and the occasional dragonfly until she got me to get over myself and join her biting at stray shadows and acting like foolish, carefree puppies.

It felt strange to throw away all boundaries, to simply be and act for the moment and not care what anyone thought. I had spent so much time since my first phase acting perfectly normal so no one would look at me askance and nobody would have the need to question whether I fit in. Now, for the first time in my life, I felt free as a wolf.

We traveled until we came to a stream, then we swam across and padded dripping wet up the other side. After that, Greg lowered his head and began to run. My feet lifted and my heart flew. I loved the feeling of my four paws hitting the ground so quickly they barely touched. The mile-eating lope of the wolf was my favorite part of turning into an animal, something else I had never been able to describe to Mom and Dad because I didn't know how they would feel if they knew how much I enjoyed phasing.

We leaped fences as swiftly as the few deer we startled and eventually left the sparse tree and meadow landscape. Open land spread before us with shrubs and low-lying plant life hiding so many rabbits and pheasants they sprang up at every turn.

Gem and I chased them until they dove into their holes or took to the air, then we searched for more while her parents wandered together across the soft, lush land. Eventually, we relaxed exhausted near the stream and lapped lazily at it while basking in the moonlight. It was enough to be close to each other, to be free, to lose the cares of the world for one night.

Before the moon set, Greg and Anna came splashing noisily back up the stream like poorly mannered puppies. Greg shoved me into the water with his shoulder, then took off up the river with Anna beside him. Gem and I ran after them. Moonlight danced within the water, beautiful and alive in silver slivers that broke into a million pieces when we loped past. A teasing breeze toyed through my fur telling of deer in a distant meadow and mice hiding among the clover at the base of a nearby tree.

Gem ran beside me, her eyes alive and a grin on her face. Our plan was to tackle her parents in the stream, but when we rounded a bend, we found them face to face with a bear. We stopped in a splash of water and barely avoided running into them.

The bear watched us with unimpressed little eyes; his massive head moved back and forth as he tested the air. A musky, earthy scent surrounded him along with the smell of the half-eaten fish on the bank nearby. Apparently Greg and

Anna had surprised him in the middle of his dinner. Greg lowered his head slightly, then began to back up. Anna did the same, forcing Gem and I to back up also or be run over.

I kept expecting the bear to charge. He looked menacing with his shaggy head and hunched shoulders. He was obviously not very pleased about his interrupted meal, but when we backed around the bend and the branches of the overhanging trees shielded us from view, I heard him pad back through the water to his fish and begin to eat again.

Greg gave me a wide-eyed look and a wolfish grin. He trotted up the bank and we followed on the long walk back to the car. The moon set before we reached the vehicles and it felt strange to stay in wolf form when I didn't have to. It was freeing, somehow, not to feel the need to phase back as soon as the moon had released its hold.

I phased on my side of the truck while Gem did the same on hers, then we both pulled on our clothes and climbed inside. As I drove, I realized how much I enjoyed sitting in silence with Gem. It felt as if the silence itself was a conversation, and a comfortable, pleasing one at that.

She finally glanced at me. "That's the first time we've ever run into a bear."

I grinned. "I believe it. I'm glad I got to be there."

"I thought it was going to attack," she said with awe in her voice.

"Me, too. I'm glad your dad knows how to handle those things."

She tipped her head at me. "What would you have done?"

I thought for a minute. "Depends on if I was hungry."

She slapped my shoulder. "You wouldn't steal fish from a bear. That's suicide."

"What if I was eating and he tried to steal the fish from me?" I asked just to see her cute, outraged look again.

HUNTER

She rewarded me with a grin that showed her dimples. "Then you give it to him," she said, emphasizing each word as if I had difficulty understanding.

"But he didn't earn it," I pointed out.

She sighed in exasperation and pushed my shoulder again, then she pillowed her head against it and propped her feet on the passenger door. She stared at the sky as it moved slowly from velvet black to satin gray to a deep, amorous purple that blanketed the earth from both ends of the horizon until it faded to a blush of pink and orange so delicate I vowed to stay up and watch more sunrises.

Her breathing quieted until she slept. I adjusted my position so that her head rested at a comfortable angle and she wouldn't wake up with a stiff neck. She said something softly that sounded like thank you and I smiled. It amazed me how comfortable I could feel with a girl leaning against my shoulder.

Somehow in the few short days we had known each other, our relationship had gone from perfect strangers to something like boyfriend and girlfriend only deeper. I felt connected to her as though we were meant to be together. I couldn't explain it, but when she smiled, happiness spread across me like the soft brush of moonlight, completing me.

I had driven a few miles enjoying the soft sound of Gem's rhythmic breathing when her body suddenly tensed. She cried out, short and sharp as though something had hit her. She sat up and stared sightlessly around, still caught in her dream. My heart ached to see her so scared. I didn't know what to do.

"Gem, it's alright," I said softly so as not to startle her. "You're with me, with Dray. You're safe."

She looked at me for several seconds, then she blinked, glanced around again, and lay back against my shoulder. I lifted my arm and when she ducked under it, I felt her body trembling. I could hear her quick, erratic breathing until it settled back into the steady rhythm of someone asleep.

I marveled at her trust after all she had been through. She was so happy and full of joy and passion even though she had gone through six months of horrible treatment, far worse than I figured she even told her parents, yet she danced and skipped and smiled as though the sun shone from inside of her instead of on the outside.

A fierce protectiveness welled up inside of me. I wouldn't let anyone else hurt her. She deserved to live a life away from pain and heartache, and away from others who meant her harm; I would do everything in my power to make that happen. I thought of the wild werewolf pack and a chill ran down my spine. Something would have to be done about them, I just didn't know what.

HUNTER

Chapter 8

"It was about time to cut your hair anyway," Mom said as she trimmed the singed ends. "It was beginning to look girly."

"Mom," I protested; we both knew she said it to make me feel better.

She shrugged. "I'm just relieved this is all that came of it. You were very brave and I'm proud of you."

I self-consciously let a hand rest on Jo's head. He wriggled happily under my touch and licked my hand. The quiet snip of the scissors sounded loud in the room until Dad stomped in from outside, a pail of fresh milk in one hand and a rusty hinge in the other. "Daisy's gone and broke the fence again. Do you have time to help me fix it before you go?"

When I got home early in the morning, he had offered to do both the feeding and the milking so I could catch up on sleep. But old habits die hard and I was up at sunrise, so I did my homework and ate, then still had plenty of time left for Mom to cut my hair. I nodded, grateful for the distraction.

I pulled on my old boots, then realized that after the fire they were my only footwear. I slipped on a pair of rubber boots instead because we would be out in the pen and my old cowboy boots stunk badly enough as it was. I grabbed my hat and followed Dad out.

Daisy chewed her cud contentedly in the corner, acting for all the world like a docile, sweet cow, when in fact the instant our backs were turned her goal was to escape her pen no matter how much damaged she caused. When we got her, Dad teased Mom about giving the cow such a generic name, but Mom said she hoped Daisy would grow up to be a generic cow. Little did we know at the time that we owned a cow Houdini.

We had replaced the same hinge three different ways

along with resetting all of the fence posts and stringing an extra strand of barbed wire across the top of the entire fence, but she still found ways to escape. She could also slip her head from the milking bar and could only be shut in the last stall because it held tighter than the rest.

"Sometimes I wonder why we keep this cow," Dad grumbled as he shoved the gate back together.

I didn't answer because no answer was needed. Mom had rescued Daisy when she was a newborn calf with an infection in her leg the dairy farmer didn't have time to bother with. Mom and Dad happened to be there on a hay sale and she saw the farmer drag the calf from the pen. They bought Daisy and Mom rode in the back of the truck beside her the whole way home.

She bottle fed the calf, treated her infection, and in return got a cow who was a good milker and docile as a puppy, but had an eye for escape and apparently adventure. The last time had her so badly tangled in barbed wire and bleeding that Dad and I almost gave up getting her out of it, but Mom wouldn't let us call it quits and we eventually managed to cut all of the wire and get her free. Mom treated her for weeks until the cow was healthy and trying to break out again.

I held the hinge while Dad nailed it back in place. He then took bailing wire and wrapped it around the hinge, twisting the wire tight to the wood so if Daisy knocked it free with her hoof, at least it would still hold enough to keep her in until we found out.

I slipped the chain back over the top of the gate and tugged it to make sure it would hold. Daisy wandered over and stuck her nose out to be petted. We both complied and the cow managed to lick Dad's hand with her long tongue. He shook his head and gave her one last scratch on the forehead. "Until next time, Daisy May."

HUNTER

We walked back to the house bathed in the early morning light. I changed my boots and hung up my hat, then ran my hands through my hair to unflatten it. I was surprised at how short it was. I let out a sigh and slung my backpack over my shoulder, then said goodbye to Mom and Dad.

Mom handed me a piece of fresh bread with jelly to eat on my way to Gem's house. By happy circumstance, she lived halfway between our home and the school, a twenty minute walk in good weather. Mom gave me a knowing smile when I told her I would rather walk than take my truck; at Dad's questioning look, she told him the walk was good for me.

I watched the sky shift from early morning burnished orange to the gold of the hundred sunflowers that lined the road and turned their faces to follow the first light of day. I took a deep breath of the morning air and held it as long as I could, enjoying the way my lungs no longer burned. When I ran down the flaming hall of the hospital gasping for air, each breath seared all the way down my trachea and I longed for morning air so fresh and clear. To have it now felt like a gift, and I tried not to take each breath for granted.

Gem ran out when I turned onto the long gravel driveway to her house and met me before I was halfway down. She slipped her arm through mine and we walked to school in pleasant silence, enjoying the call of the meadow larks and final songs of the crickets before they settled in for the day. I was loath to give up the peace of our walk, but school loomed into view all too soon and the magic of the morning was broken.

***

Apparently saving a car from a train and rescuing patients from a burning hospital were enough to make a person a celebrity in Thistle. Two different couples pulled their cars over when they passed Gem and I on our way to school and got out to ask us what had happened and to commend me on my bravery. I asked Gem after they left why no one mentioned her own courage, but she just laughed and skipped backwards in front of me.

"It helps that my dad got a job at the newspaper," she said lightly.

"Couldn't you have asked him to leave me out of the story also?" I replied.

She shook her head. "This town needs a hero, Dray Dawson, and that hero is you."

I rolled my eyes. "I want to live a normal life."

"Normal like Clark Kent, or normal like Bruce Wayne?" I moved to grab her and she danced out of my reach, grinning and laughing. "With great power comes great responsibility."

This time I laughed. "You watch way too many superhero movies."

She shook her head. "I read way too many comic books. They're more captivating."

Preston burst out of the school and ran up to us. "Is it true you saved like fifty people from the hospital fire?"

I sighed while Gem laughed. "No, I helped get three patients out, but Gem was there, and so were the firefighters and-"

He cut me off without listening. "The whole school's talking about it! Scotty says his dad wants to give you a car just for the publicity."

"I don't need a car," I protested. "I like my truck."

Preston held open the door and waved us in with a

flourish. "My lord, my lady."

I sighed, but Gem strode in as if she owned the school. She directed everyone's questions to me, even going so far as to say that she just waited at the window while I did all of the hard work. By the time I reached first period History, I had heard four different accounts of how I saved more than twenty people, including two firefighters, and helped hose down the hospital afterwards.

Gem left me at the door with a cheerful goodbye. "Enjoy," she said with a laugh. I rolled my eyes as she skipped away toward her Algebra class.

I pushed through the people at the door and slumped into a seat in the back corner, but Mr. Andrews had apparently been waiting for me to enter. He followed me to my desk and stood silently until I looked up to see tears in his usually stern brown eyes. "My mother was one of the people you pulled from that fire," he said, his voice tight.

My heart caught. The gratitude and relief on his face shone starkly against the neon lights overhead. For the first time I saw the fire as others must see it. I saw the lives in the flames, those saved and those lost, and realized that by going in there I really had made a difference.

I rose and held out a hand. "I was glad to do it."

Mr. Andrews ignored my hand and gave me a quick hug, then stepped back. "I know that was against the policies and procedures manual, but I promised my wife I would give you a hug for her, so thank you."

"I would gladly do it again," I said.

He looked at me seriously, then patted me on the shoulder. "I believe you would. Bruce is a friend of mine. He was one of the firefighters who helped bring the patients down, and he told me what really happened. I don't know if many could truly say they would do it again."

I thought of the fire and the way the air was so hot it burned my eyes. The smoke snaked down my throat as if trying to choke me from the inside out, and the floor moved as I walked, a living carpet of flame. The thought of facing something like that again sent a finger of adrenaline rushing through my veins, but I would. If lives were at stake, I wouldn't hesitate.

Mr. Andrews began teaching, but threw me another grateful look when the bell rang and we left class. I met Gem in English. Mrs. Moody dove deep into Macbeth and didn't notice the class whispering back and forth. About halfway through the period, the intercom buzzed and Principal McCormick said, "Please send Dray Dawson to my office."

Students speculated and Gem gave me a questioning look with one raised eyebrow. I shrugged and rose, taking my backpack with me in case whatever he needed took longer than the class period. I closed the classroom door and loud talking erupted behind me. Mrs. Moody called for everyone to quiet down and silence followed me up the hall.

I walked into the office I had avoided my whole life. The charming smile of the school secretary, Ms. Crenshaw, met me at the door. She tipped her head to indicate that I could go straight back. I walked slowly down the hall to a modest office on the right with the name tag 'Principal Jethro McCormick' on the door. It was open a crack and creaked open further when I knocked.

"Come in," the Principal called.

I opened the door all the way; Principal McCormick made a few notes on a pad of paper before he glanced up and saw me. "Have a seat," he said with a warm smile that eased some of my trepidation.

I sat in one of the two brown, hardback chairs on the other side of the desk and studied him. I had seen him around the school often and at assemblies, but I had never been face to face with the man. He was shorter than me with a rotund figure and kind eyes behind dark blue-rimmed glasses. He held his pencil correctly and there were no chew marks on the yellow painted wood or the eraser. He sat straight and wrote as though he enjoyed it. I waited quietly and tried not to fidget.

The Principal finished whatever he was working on, then smoothed the pages back down on the yellow pad and set it on the corner of his desk so that it aligned perfectly with the wood. He sharpened his yellow pencil in the electric sharpener on the other corner of the desk, then placed the pencil back in a cup with five other sharpened pencils. The cup proudly proclaimed, "PrinciPAL of the Year," and had been signed by the school staff.

Principal McCormick laced his fingers together on top of his desk and looked at me. "Mr. Dawson, I know of you but we haven't had the pleasure of a formal meeting."

I held out a hand. "Nice to meet you officially, sir."

He shook my hand, then nodded at the newspaper on the top of his neatly organized paper tray. "I read about the fire this morning." His cheerful demeanor faded slightly. "That was a bad business. It's a shame something like that happened and I hope they get to the bottom of it."

His words caught my attention. "Do they think it was started on purpose?"

He nodded solemnly. "From what I've heard, the flames spread too quickly to be natural. There wasn't time to contain the fire before it had the entire place lit, and the sprinklers never went on, an indication of tampering."

I hadn't thought about the sprinklers. They would have been nice; the fact that they were disabled showed more foresight to the fire than I had realized.

Principal McCormick cleared his throat and straightened. "Anyway, I wanted to thank you personally for the valor you showed, and for the example you are to the other students here at Thistle High. I would like to arrange for a medal-"

I shook my head quickly. "No thank you, sir. I really don't think that's necessary."

His shaggy eyebrows lifted. "Are you sure? It'd be good for the rest of the students to see you get commended for your bravery."

I shook my head again. "No, sir. Please. I did what I could and I wasn't alone. There are others who deserve a medal more than I, and I really don't want to be singled out."

The Principal studied me for a minute, then a smile touched the corners of his lips. "Alright, but you deserve it. If you're certain?" When I nodded, he gave a short, dismissive sigh. "Very well. But if you change your mind, let me know." He pulled the pad of paper back out and flipped open to his previous page.

"I will. Thank you, sir." I rose, then hesitated. "Am I, uh, alright to go?"

"Hmmm?" He glanced up, then nodded. "Oh yes, of course. Thank you for coming in." He held out his hand and I shook it again, then retreated quickly from the office.

HUNTER

***

Preston, Scotty, and I ran laps, then went outside with the others to play flag football. Coach Matthews contrived to have Preston and I play against each other at quarterback. I threw several tight spirals, then saw the Coach watching closely and threw ducks on the next two. He pursed his lips like he was holding in a laugh, completely unconvinced.

I ran in with the others after class, changed out of my gym clothes, and was ready to leave when I saw him at the gym door talking to Tim, the captain of the wrestling team. I pushed Preston and Scotty forward, hoping to sneak by, but Coach Matthews spotted us.

"Mr. Dawson?"

I cringed inwardly. "I'll catch up," I told my friends, then walked back to the door.

"Enjoy playing quarterback?" he asked with a knowing smile.

I shrugged. "It was alright," I said to cover up the fact that I had been ecstatic when I was chosen.

He leaned forward conspiratorially. "You know, you don't have to pull people from a fire to get attention."

I forced a laugh. "Thanks, Coach. I'll keep that in mind."

He motioned toward the door. "Have a good day, Mr. Dawson."

"Thank you, Coach." I hurried to catch up to Preston and Scotty, grateful to have gotten off so easily while a part of me reasoned that he was doing a good job of trying to break me down.

Chapter 9

Gem met me after my seventh period Art class. Scotty eyed her suspiciously, but Preston grinned when he caught up to us after his History class. "Hi, Gem," he said, blushing.

"Hi, Preston. How was your day?"

Preston looked around and stammered, "It was, uh, well, it was good."

"That's great," Gem replied with a kind smile. "I'm glad to hear it." She slipped her arm into mine and Scotty gave me a suspicious look.

"If you want that car, Dad says to come over and get it," he said, smoothing his hair and avoiding looking at Gem entirely.

I sighed. "Tell him thanks, but the truck works just fine so he can give it to someone else."

He stared at me. "He'll put it back on the lot and sell it. It's a free car, Dray."

Foreboding thoughts rose to my mind and I swallowed a lump in my throat. "People died in that fire. I don't want a car from it when others lost loved ones."

Scotty looked taken aback. "I didn't think of it like that."

I put a hand on his shoulder. "Your dad was trying to be nice."

"And capitalize on an investment opportunity," Preston pointed out.

"Please tell him I appreciate it," I concluded, ignoring Preston. "It was a nice gesture regardless, but I really do like my truck."

"If you're into run-down antiques not worth anything," Scotty conceded with his movie star smile.

Gem grinned. "I like it. It has charm."

"The charm of a rusted bucket," Scotty agreed.

"See you guys tomorrow," I said.

Gem twiddled her fingers in a wave. "See ya fellas."

Preston returned her wave happily, but Scotty sulked and ignored her.

"He's nice," she said dryly when they were out of earshot, her eyes bright and mischievous.

"I would say he means well, but he doesn't," I replied.

Gem slipped her arm contentedly through mine. The warm sun bathed her in light and I wondered again how I had gotten so lucky as to have her walking beside me.

We ambled in comfortable silence toward her home and I was escorting her to the door when a scent caught my attention. I glanced up and saw that the front door was partially open. Trepidation filled my chest. I caught Gem's arm. "Stay here," I said.

"What's wrong?" She looked at the house, then her nostrils flared and panic fill her eyes. "Mom, Dad!" she yelled. She yanked her arm out of my grasp and ran for the front door.

I took off after her, afraid of what she would find. The inside of the house was destroyed. Lamps were broken, the couch ripped to pieces, pictures torn from the walls, the table and chairs smashed, and the carpet covered in what smelled like werewolf urine and refuse. Gem ran past it all without pause and I followed her upstairs to find both her parents on the floor of the master bedroom.

Gem let out a little squeak of fear and fell to her knees beside her mom. She rolled her over gently and Anna let out a little, pained breath. "Gem?" she asked softly.

I ran to Greg. He sat with his back against the wall and his chin on his chest; he held a baseball bat in one hand that was covered in blood on the end. His chest rose and fell and when I touched his arm, his hand tightened on the bat. "It's alright, Greg, it's me, Dray. What happened?"

He blinked, then stared wildly at his wife and Gem. His gaze calmed when he saw them talking. "The werewolves," he said, then he doubled over and began to cough. Blood colored his lips when he stopped and he clutched his side. I checked under his shirt and found deep, bleeding bite marks down his ribs to his stomach.

I grabbed towels from the bathroom, handed several to Gem, then used mine to wrap Greg's wounds. My hands shook so hard with outrage by the time I was done I could barely dial our phone number on the Hawthornes' phone. "Mom, where's Dad?" I asked quickly.

The tone of my voice kept her from asking questions and a few seconds later I heard Dad hurry into the room. "What's going on, Dray?" he asked.

"Dad, the werewolf pack attacked the Hawthornes. I need you guys to get over here right away."

I heard Mom gasp in the background. Dad told her to get the farm medical bag, then said, "We'll be there in a minute."

I hung up the phone and watched Gem carefully bandage huge gashes in her mom's leg, stomach, and arms. I couldn't think past a red rage that filled me so intensely I could barely breathe.

"Why would they do this?" Gem asked quietly. She glanced up at me and tears streaked her cheeks. "Why attack my parents?"

"They're trying to tell us they don't have any limits." The truth beat through my heart and multiplied my anger. "They're saying they can ruin our lives if we mess with them."

Gem shook her head. "It isn't right. Mom and Dad didn't do anything." Anna winced as her daughter bandaged a particularly painful wound; tears flowed down Gem's cheeks. "This isn't right," she said in a strangled voice that made my heart pound harder.

I wanted to go to the werewolves and show them what would happen if they messed with my town, with my friends, and, I glanced at Gem, with the girl I loved. I clenched my fists, wanting more than anything to tear into the pack and make them pay for thinking they could hurt people without consequences.

"I'm going to call Jaze," Gem said. She ran from the room and I heard her dial.

I knelt beside Greg and checked the towels. They were holding, but with the amount of wounds they had suffered, Gem's parents would heal slowly. Blood loss and stress would slow it down even more. Blood stained the floor beneath both of them.

"Can you take me to Anna?" Greg asked softly; the weakness of his voice betrayed the true extent of his injuries. I slipped an arm under his knees and another under his shoulders, then stood up as carefully as I could. Greg winced, but kept silent.

I carried him to Anna's side, then lowered him gently to the carpet next to her. Anna opened her eyes, caught Greg's hand in hers, then closed her eyes again. "Are you alright?" she asked quietly.

He nodded. "I am now."

Tears filled my eyes. I turned away from them. Gem talked quickly to her werewolf friends on the phone. I heard their shock, then their promise that they would leave immediately. Gem's voice shook when she spoke to Jaze and told him how badly her parents were hurt and how afraid she was.

Help was on the way. I couldn't control my rage any longer. I pushed open the window next to the Hawthornes' bed and jumped out. I ran as soon as my feet hit the ground.

My parents were on their way, the Hawthornes would be alright, but I couldn't guarantee the safety of Gem, my parents, my friends, or anyone in Thistle with a pack of wild werewolves in our backyard who had no qualms about hurting innocent people.

In my mind I saw Gem kneeling on the floor next to her mother, her blue eyes wide with helplessness, her long sleeves pushed up to her elbows, and her mother's blood covering the dark stripes from the silver whips across her arms. I had promised that I would never let her get hurt again, never let her worry that the people she loved were in danger; the werewolves had destroyed that promise in one rash act, and I wanted to make them pay for their actions.

Fury filled me until I couldn't take it anymore. I ripped off my clothes and phased, then ran through the woods faster than I ran with the Hawthornes. My paws barely touched the ground, my dark gray fur rippled with the touch of the breeze, and I leaped each barbed wire fence without slowing. I tore through the Jamison's field, into the Anderson's, then jumped the wide canal that separated their fields from the Parker's and flew over the fence to the wooded area at the base of the hill.

I slowed when I reached the trees and trotted warily toward the smell of werewolf, blood, animal refuse, and garbage. Most of the werewolves were still in their wolf form from attacking Gem's family. Several lowered their heads and stalked out to meet me even before I entered their trash-strewn clearing.

Blankets, cardboard boxes, and a tarp made up what they might consider a sleeping area; a smoldering fire lay in a poorly dug fire pit, and a despicable amount of garbage from soda cans, pizza boxes, fast food packaging, cans of soup, boxes of pastries and sweets, half-eaten fruit, and cans of beer littered the ground everywhere I looked. The clearing smelled of trash, sewage, and filthy, unwashed bodies.

Disgust filled my eyes and the werewolves bristled. Two of the eight member pack were in their human form. "Get our message?" the tall, skinny one with the scratches on his face sneered. He had a tattoo of a wolf across his chest. I rolled my eyes, wishing I could tell him how stupid it looked.

I growled and the sneer wiped from his face at the vehemence in it. All of the anger and helplessness I had felt in the hospital fire and tending to Gem's parents rolled in my chest and came out as pure hatred, undiluted and ready for vengeance. The skinny werewolf threw down the beer he had been drinking and phased. Adrenaline rushed through my veins and I charged.

Even though a few of the werewolves had darker coats then mine and were therefore according to Gem closer to Alpha strength, the anger that pumped adrenaline through my veins made me stronger and faster. I darted in and out, slicing and slashing, then backing up so they couldn't get behind me. Rain began to fall, a soft patter on the ground countering the snarls, yelps, and growls.

I grabbed the skinny werewolf's shoulder and bit down. My teeth grated against bone and he howled, then another werewolf bit my leg and I had to drop him to defend myself. I bit at the werewolf's stomach, ducked under another attempting to tear out my throat, then jumped and landed on a different werewolf's back. I grabbed the back of his neck in my jaws, then rolled to the side and threw him into two others. I charged at two more and bowled them over, then left a series of deep slashes along the first one's ribs before he could rise.

I was only one against eight, and as the anger faded I began to realize the mistake I had made thinking I could take on eight grays with only vengeance to fuel me. Bites began to hurt, teeth held on longer before I could break away, and as my own blood started to flow, my reactions slowed and my strength began to fade. The werewolves ganged up on me, a pack now defending their own territory against a lone wolf who came to hurt them. I backed up to a tree with low-swept branches to protect my back, but they got through my guard anyway. There were too many of them for me to defend myself.

The rain turned into a downpour. My actions had been stupid, careless, and now I was alone to face my own consequences. I squinted against the rain, trying to dodge the attacks when they came. I slipped in the slick mud and went down on my side. Two werewolves took advantage of the situation and bit at my ribs and stomach, leaving deep lacerations before I could get back to my feet. I tried to back around the tree, but other werewolves were there waiting for me. They were going to kill me; the realization made my blood run cold.

I gritted my teeth and dodged another attempt at my throat. My movements were short and halting, and he managed to tear a good chunk out of my chest. My choices rushed through my head, a quick list that began with giving up and letting them kill me, and ended with running away like a coward, with nothing in between. My wolf instincts called for survival, but I wasn't a coward. I kept repeating the words over and over in my head. I wasn't a coward, and I wouldn't let them win after what they had done.

A small voice in the back of my mind said that I couldn't win the battle I had picked. I argued against it and fought tooth to tooth when a werewolf grew bold and attacked head-on. I thought of my parents and how much they believed in me despite what I had turned into.

HUNTER

I pushed the werewolf back, snapping at its front paws and making it dance out of the way. I saw Gem again and heard the words I had promised her in my truck when she confessed her fear of the fire. "You'll never have to worry like that again. I promise I'll always come back, no matter what." The words felt ironic now that I was about to break them.

I let out an enraged growl, leapt forward like I was ready to take them all on again, then turned and ran as fast as my battered body would let me.

The werewolves chased me through the fields, blood streaming down my sides and my breath short and painful. I thought they were going to catch me, then one by one they dropped off. I leaped over the fences, took a path straight up the Tayne River where two more werewolves left, darted across the Anderson's field and lost one werewolf between stacks of ton bales, then leaped the fence at Jamison's. My feet gave out when I landed.

I rolled and hit up hard against a hay bale. The last werewolf gave me a toothy wolf grin. He dove for my stomach, but I jumped out of the way at the last minute and he smashed into the bale. I grabbed the side of his neck and forced him to the ground. I worried at the skin and felt it shred. The werewolf whined, then used more strength than I had to pull himself free. He shot me an enraged glare, then ran back to the fence, jumped it, and limped through the fields out of sight.

I panted hard, trying to catch my breath. The lacerations along my ribs burned and the cold chill from the rain made me shiver. I tried to stand up, but my legs wouldn't hold and I collapsed back to the ground. Blood ran to the new alfalfa growing under my paws and I shook uncontrollably. I huddled against the hay bale for protection against the pounding rain, but it did little to slow the water or my chills.

I remembered when our dog Jo sliced his paw on the screen door and kept licking the wound. Mom told me it helped to stop the bleeding and start the cut healing. I grimaced at the thought, but figured it couldn't hurt. I licked what I could of my wounds, and the pain did ease a bit. The rain slowed and my body shuddered. I hoped the rain would hinder the werewolves if they decided to regroup and come after me while I was weak.

Minutes drifted into an hour and the rain began to let up. I shivered and couldn't fight the phase any longer. My body changed back to human form and the wounds which had begun to close opened and tore with the different shape. I yelled, but the rain covered the weak sound.

I fell back to the ground and laughed bitterly at my pathetic state. How was I supposed to protect anyone when I couldn't defend the family of the girl I loved? How were they ever going to be safe when the werewolf pack could do so much damage in such a short time? My thoughts blended together and I stared at the falling rain.

HUNTER

Chapter 10

"Dray?"

A voice broke through my daze. I had no idea what time it was, but the sun had set and left me in darkness. I pushed up slightly, sure I was hearing things; then it sounded again.

"Dray, are you out here?"

I squinted through the darkness. The sound of footsteps brought me to my knees. I coughed the rainwater from my lungs and the motion tore pain through my body. I coughed again and again, unable to stop until only the hay bale kept me up.

"Dray?"

Several people ran in my direction. I hunched against the hay, worried that the werewolves had found me and would finish the job. The thought sent a surge of adrenaline through my body. I leaped at the first person who came around the bale.

The werewolf I attacked swiftly sidestepped, then used my motion to propel me into the ground where I lay gasping for air. He looked down at me with cold, calculating dark blue eyes. Rain dripped down his black hair and he clenched and unclenched his fists as if hoping I would attack again.

"Great, Jet. Just what he needed," another werewolf muttered, kneeling next to me. He found me still alert and gave me a friendly smile. "At least he didn't kill you. It's a bad habit." He spread a blanket over the lower half of my body, then began to check my wounds.

Both werewolves exuded a sense of power and confidence I hadn't experienced before. It took only one look at the way they met my eyes, the cast of their jaws, and the line of their shoulders to know they were both Alphas.

I tried to sit up, but the Alpha next to me held me down.

"Give me a chance to look these over. I can't have you dying on the way home from blood loss." His gaze took in all my wounds as though he had seen many of the same before. He looked older than me by only about two years, but his gaze was aged as though he had seen too many things to be young anymore. He began to wrap the worst of my wounds in bandages.

I swallowed a cry of pain when he touched a gash in my abdomen. Jaze frowned and glanced at another werewolf behind him. I followed his eyes to an older boy with startling dark red eyes. He watched the fields around us expectantly as if almost hoping the pack would show up.

I winced at a knife of pain along my ribs. "Sorry. They got you good." A hint of humor touched the Alpha's brown eyes. "I'm Jaze, by the way, and this is Jet," he nodded at the one who had taken me down as though I was less bother than a fly. "And that's Kaynan."

I hissed in a breath at another jab of pain and sat up, tired of being prodded. "You're Gem's friends?" At his nod, I frowned. "I thought you were in Texas. How'd you get here so fast?"

Jaze smiled. "The newest addition to our arsenal happens to be a jet. It makes these trips a bit quicker."

I stared at him. "You own a private jet?"

He shrugged. "We never know where we're going to be needed quickly." He gave me a pointed look. "It's especially handy in situations like these."

I wrapped the blanket more securely around my waist and tried to rise. When I stumbled, Jaze and Kaynan caught me. "Take it easy, kid," Kaynan said, his red eyes creating a demonic counterbalance to his quick smile. "You've got to give these things time."

"Which we don't have," Jaze replied. "He's right to get

moving. That pack's not going to let him get off easy after what we've seen. They really like to leave an impression."

"I'll leave an impression," Jet said softly in a voice edged with steel.

Jaze shook his head. "We need to find out what's going on here first. I want you to find them and arrange a meeting."

Jet looked like he would rather just kill them all, but he shrugged and disappeared into the rainy night. Kaynan and Jaze helped me walk back to the house. Blood from my lesser wounds mixed with the rain, but the major few had responded to Jaze's bandaging and were already starting to heal. By the time we reached my backyard, the pain had lessened and was replaced with a terrible exhaustion that filled every inch of my body.

"It's not every day I see one werewolf try to take on a pack by himself." Jaze glanced at me. "I can't decide if you're foolhardy or brave."

I gritted my teeth against a stab of pain. "I'm going with foolhardy."

Jaze chuckled and helped me stand somewhat steadily. "I'd recommend walking in on your own power if you can. It'll be easier on Gem and your parents."

I nodded and pulled open the screen door. Jo barked, then ran down the hallway, skidded across the kitchen linoleum, and bounced up and down in front of me. His tongue was out and his brown eyes were so happy to see me that I knelt gingerly and let him lick me while I ran my hands through his silky hair. His enthusiasm gave me the strength to face my family. I took a steeling breath, then rose and walked slowly into the living room.

Mom and Dad rose from the couch and hurried over to me while Jo bounced past and began to sniff at Jaze and Kaynan.

"Oh, Dray, what were you thinking?" Mom asked. She looked me over, her eyes bright with concern at the bite marks.

"He was protecting his territory," Jaze said from behind me. "And he did a good job, from what I could tell."

I threw him a grateful look. He just smiled and excused himself to check on Gem's parents.

"Are you alright?" Dad asked uncertainly.

I glanced down at my rain-soaked, cut-up body. The bandages Jaze put on had bled through and looked a lot worse than I actually felt. I gave my parents a reassuring smile. "I'm fine. It's not as bad as it looks."

I peeled away a bandage from across my stomach. Mom tried to stop me, but when the bandage came off to reveal an already healing gash washed clean by the rain, her expression softened. "Let's clean those properly so you don't get an infection." She hurried off to the bedroom. I was about to follow when Dad stopped me.

"You, uh, might want proper attire to check on Gem and her family." He gave me a meaningful look that made me realize I wasn't wearing more than a rain-soaked blanket.

"Oh, right," I said. Dad chuckled and led the way to my room. I couldn't remember the last time he had been in there. He was very intent on giving me my privacy, saying that a growing boy deserved his own personal space, so when he shut the door behind him and occupied himself studying the posters on my walls, I knew he was truly concerned.

I pulled on a pair of loose cotton pants and grabbed a white tee-shirt, then changed my mind and selected a black button-up shirt instead. If the wounds still bled the dark color would hide it, and I wasn't sure I could get a shirt over my head anyway.

Trying to hide the weakness that made me so tired I

could barely stand, I sat on the bed to button my shirt. My fingers trembled and it was hard to put the buttons through the holes. Dad turned, then sat on the bed beside me and buttoned up the shirt. It ate at my pride that I needed help with something so simple, but I was grateful for the assistance.

"It's been a long time since I've done this," he said with a touch of humor to his voice.

"It's been a long time since I've needed it," I replied. I took a breath, then winced when it pulled at the lacerations along my ribs.

Dad paused and glanced at me. "You know, your mom and I are grateful that you found other werewolves and can feel normal, but," he turned his attention back to the buttons, "I don't know if it's worth it."

His words stung with truth. I studied the floor. "Gem's family had nothing to do with this, but none of it would have happened if the wild werewolf pack had stayed away. It's hard to control my instincts knowing they're hurting people."

He sat back and picked up a frame from the dresser by my bed. The photo showed Dad and I throwing a baseball to each other over the hen house. I had a big grin on my face and my towhead blond hair stuck up everywhere. Dad wore overalls, work boots, and a straw cowboy hat on his head. Tools sat on the ground near the half-finished coup and it was obvious we had found something more entertaining to occupy our time than completing the hen house.

"You're a good person, Dray," Dad said, studying the picture. "It's good to help others when you can." He gave me a serious look, "But even you have limits." Something dark crossed his eyes and he turned back to the picture. "When Gem told us you went after the wolf pack, we didn't know what to think, but when Jaze got here and heard, he and the others took off after you so fast I'm sure they thought they would find you dead."

I swallowed at the stifled emotions in his voice. "I'm sorry, Dad."

He nodded. "I know, and Ma does, too. But you can't protect everyone."

I gestured in the direction of the guest bedroom. "I can't even protect those I care about."

He put an arm around my shoulder in a rare gesture and sighed. "Tell me about it."

I gave him a wry grin and he smiled back. "At least you get what I'm talking about."

I rose slowly, then grabbed the bedpost when my knees threatened to give out. Dad's eyes colored with concern. "Are you sure you should get up?"

"I need to check on Greg and Anna," I replied.

"And Gem?" he hazarded. I nodded and he smiled. "She seems nice."

"She's amazing," I said. I took a breath, then admitted, "I think I'm falling for her."

He nodded as if he had guessed as much. "I think she's worth falling for."

He held open the door to my room and I walked slowly past him. He followed me back to the living room where Mom waited with her bandages. "I don't really need them, Mom," I pointed out.

"Humor her," Dad whispered behind me. "She needs to feel like she can help."

I gave in and sat on the chair she indicated. She unbuttoned my shirt; Dad and I both sighed at that. She checked the wounds across my stomach and chest, cleaned them with warm water and a rage, and applied salve to a few of them. She then motioned for me to lift the back of my shirt. She clicked her tongue at whatever she found there and put on a few bandages, then came back around and did up the buttons without waiting for me to ask. "That's as good as I can do. At least they're clean now and can heal without getting an infection."

I chose not to ask if werewolves could get infections and stood just as Gem came out of the guest room where her parents were staying. She looked up, saw me, then ran down the hall faster than I had ever seen her move. She almost flew into my arms, then stopped inches from me and hesitated.

"Are you alright?" she asked, her eyes searching my face. Her fingers fluttered at her sides like humming birds as though she wanted to touch me but wasn't sure if she should. Mom and Dad slipped casually out of the room, Mom's hand secure in Dad's.

I nodded. "Nothing a good night's sleep won't fix. How are your parents?"

She sighed and it was a heartbreaking sound that reminded me of why I had gone after the pack to begin with. It told of hidden places damaged that might never heal, and of the fear that the near loss of a loved one can bring. "They're healing, but not quickly. The pack got them pretty bad."

I nodded at her understatement. "They're strong."

She mistook my meaning. "You shouldn't have gone against them. They're too powerful."

I gritted my teeth. "No one should be able to hurt others and get away with it."

She looked at the floor. "I guess I've just seen it so often that it's easier to run away." Her voice cracked. "I've never been able to fight back and make a difference."

"That's not true."

I bristled at the new werewolf who walked down the hall.

He was huge, one of the biggest guys I had ever seen. He had dark blond hair and brown eyes, and met Gem's gaze with a familiarity that made the hair rise on the back of my neck. The way he held himself told that he was an Alpha. I was beginning to feel like there were too many Alphas in my home.

"You certainly made a difference to me," he continued. He glanced at me, friendly and casual, then looked away so he wouldn't challenge me in my own home. It was then that I noticed the stripes that ran up his arms, black marks like Gem's. He wore a short-sleeved shirt as if daring anyone to question him about them. I took a calming breath. "You're Vance."

He nodded. "Gem saved my life." He looked at her. "You can't honestly say you haven't made a difference."

She gestured toward the bedroom and tears shone bright in her eyes. "What good does it matter if my own parents are hurt because of me?"

Vance and I both shook our heads. "It's not your fault there's a wild werewolf pack in our town," I pointed out. "That could've happened anywhere."

"No werewolf could take on a pack that size alone," Vance continued. "Look at Dray."

We both stared at him, then I started to laugh. Vance laughed with me, relieved that I could take a joke. My sides ached. I held my ribs and lowered myself into the easy chair. "I look that bad, huh?"

Gem put a hand softly on my cheek. "It was foolish to go after them."

I looked away from her knowing blue eyes. "Tell me about it."

Vance settled onto the couch across from us. "It was brave. Not many Alphas I know would have gone against eight wild werewolves by themselves, let alone a gray coat."

Jaze, Jet, and Kaynan walked in from the kitchen. "That's for certain," Jaze agreed.

I was glad everyone knew of my stupidity. I dangled a hand for Jo to lick.

"The meeting's set," Jaze said. The depth to his tone indicated it would be a challenging one.

"What time?" Gem asked with dread.

Jaze glanced at Jet. "Now," the black-haired Alpha said simply. He leaned against the door frame, his arms at his sides and dark eyes on the windows. His fists clenched and unclenched slowly.

Kaynan, the one with the strange red eyes, cleaned a knife with a rag, then somehow clasped the knife to his wrist. The knife locked in a strange circular pattern, looking for all the world like an armband.

Jaze turned from Gem to me. "I'm leaving Vance here for protection. I'll need Jet and Kaynan in case there's trouble."

"We'll be alright," Gem said resolutely. She sat on the arm of the easy chair and slipped her hand into mine.

"I need to be there," I said, surprising myself. The heavy weariness that filled my body recommended otherwise, but I wasn't about to sit and let other werewolves fight my battle for me.

Jaze shook his head. "If you don't mind, I'd rather you sit this one out." His gaze said he guessed more of my weakness than I let on. He continued, "We're going for a peace talk and it would be better not to bring someone they've already had a quarrel with."

"They're in my territory, and I don't want them to think they can walk over this town and get away with it."

Jaze glanced at Jet. The dark-haired werewolf didn't take his eyes off me. "You'd do the same thing," he quietly.

Jaze's eyebrows lifted in surprise and a hint of a smile showed on his face. He let out a breath. "This is your territory and your home. I won't argue with you." He studied me carefully, then said, "But I'm calling the shots."

"Deal," I agreed.

Gem's fingers tightened in mine. She wouldn't dispute my decision, but she was worried. "You really think a peace talk is going to work?" she asked doubtfully.

Jaze met both of our eyes. "You're certain they started the hospital fire." At our nod, he continued grimly, "Then their actions have killed people. We'll mark them with trackers and force them to leave. If they go anywhere near civilization again, we'll know about it and they'll have to answer to the Hunters."

He studied me. "Can you be ready to leave in five minutes?"

I nodded. He hesitated like he wanted to say something, then turned away and left the room; Jet disappeared after him. Gem gave me a searching look. "Are you sure you want to do this?"

"I won't fight," I promised her. We both knew I wasn't in any shape for another brawl. "But I won't let them think they can threaten this town without consequences. I need to be there."

I rose gingerly and went to my bedroom. I pulled on jeans and a thick jacket, then as an afterthought sprayed some cologne on my clothes so they wouldn't smell the blood from my healing wounds. A sound by the door made me turn. The huge werewolf, Vance, stood in the doorway watching me.

"Masking the scent of blood is a good idea." His eyes narrowed thoughtfully. "Wild werewolf packs are like sharks. If they smell weakness, they devour everything in their path."

"I'm not weak," I said quietly.

He shook his head. "No, you're not." He glanced over his shoulder, then gestured into the room. "May I?"

I hadn't realized he stood at the threshold out of respect for my territory. I hesitated.

"You're about to go chasing after those werewolves which leaves me in charge of protecting your home," he pointed out. "Now would probably be a good time for some trust."

I studied him. "Why should I trust you?"

A shadow of a smile crossed his face. He stepped into the room and pulled the door shut behind him. At my apprehensive expression, he smiled. "Look, Dray. You may be foolish for going after that pack by yourself, but I respect the heck out of you for doing it. Wolves protect their territories, but they usually have a pack behind them to uphold their rights. You did it on your own. That took guts."

Surprised, I watched him warily. "Uh, thanks?"

He leaned against the door and shoved his hands in his pockets. The werewolf dwarfed my room. "I just wanted to say thanks for taking care of Gem. She needs a friend after what she's been through."

I bristled at the word friend. I wasn't sure what she thought of me, but I felt like we were so much more than just friends. "She's great," I said carefully.

He grinned as if he guessed what I was holding back. "Amazing, more like it. She's the strongest person I've ever met." His gaze darkened slightly. "Did she tell you what happened to her?" He gestured at his arms. "How she got these?"

I shook my head. "Her mom told me a bit."

He fell quiet for a minute, his eyes on the carpet. When he spoke again, he didn't look up. "There's so much more I know she wouldn't tell anyone. It was the worst experience of my life." He met my eyes, his own serious and with a depth of pain I couldn't comprehend. "She carried me through it, Dray. That little wisp of a girl was stronger than every other werewolf caught in those cages." A glimmer of challenge showed in his eyes. "And she trusts me."

I watched him standing there, an Alpha who was taking the time to make sure I felt comfortable about him protecting my family. Gem trusted him. I nodded. "If Gem trusts you, I trust you."

He smiled. "That might be the smartest thing you've said tonight."

I laughed and hide a wince at the answering pain that jolted through my ribs. I asked a question that had been bothering me. "If Alphas are so dominant, how do so many of you work together?"

Vance thought about it for a minute. "We're all in it to help werewolves. That's what Alphas are for." He shrugged. "And we all owe Jaze in some way. He's done so much for the werewolves in this country that if he calls for a favor, everyone's eager to respond. You're lucky he's here."

Vance opened the door and waited until I passed, then he followed me out. "I have a girlfriend," he said in an undertone. I glanced back at him and he lifted an eyebrow. "So you don't have to worry about competition with Gem."

"Who says you're competition?" I shot back.

He gave a deep laugh and followed me into the living room where Jaze and Kaynan waited.

"Jet's staking out our meeting place," Jaze told me. "He'll meet us there." He glanced at Vance. "Call us if anything suspicious happens."

"It's not like I'll need the help," Vance said with a grin. He flexed more muscles than I knew a person could possess.

Jaze rolled his eyes. "Just call."

HUNTER

Vance laughed and opened the door for us. I was grateful Dad and Mom weren't there to try to stop me. I felt guilty about leaving them again, but I couldn't sit back and let the others fight my battle. I might have been beaten, but I wouldn't give up until Thistle was safe.

Chapter 11

We walked across the soaked fields and through the fence following the path Gem and I had taken. Jaze paused at the tree line and a black form detached itself from the shadows. "Any problems?" Jaze questioned.

Jet shook his head. "They're waiting."

Jaze nodded. "Good." He took a step forward, then turned. "Remember, we're here to negotiate their removal from Thistle, not to fight."

Kaynan let out a snort. "If I recall correctly, we've never had a peaceful negotiation in regards to removal from someone's territory."

Jaze studied the trees around us. "There's always a first time." He led the way to the werewolves' camp. I hung back as planned so I wouldn't trigger a fight just by being there.

The werewolves were waiting for us amid the filth and litter they claimed as their campground. Four of them were in wolf form while the other four waited as scraggly, dirty humans. The one with matted brown hair and scratches on his face that I recognized from our first trip to the camp stepped forward. "You summoned us?" he asked with a sneer.

Jaze's expression was calm, but Jet and Kaynan paced on each side in order to protect him should the werewolves turn hostile. "I'm Jaze Carso, and these are my friends, Jet, Kaynan, and you've already met Dray."

The werewolf's eyes bored into mine. I met his stare and refused to show any weakness from my injuries. "I'm Terence," he said with a growl. The word sounded unfamiliar from his tongue, as though it had been a long time since he had responded to it.

"Jet told you the reason for our visit," Jaze said with an

amiable smile.

The werewolf glowered. "He said our presence was unwelcome."

Jaze nodded. "You injured and killed humans in the fire you started in the hospital, and your pack also attacked two werewolves in their own home. These actions are unacceptable."

"Who's to say it was us?" Terence questioned with a quirked eyebrow and a smile that was contrary to his dangerous tone. Several of the werewolves around him laughed.

Jaze's eyes narrowed. "You weren't exactly trying to hide your tracks."

Terence shrugged. "There were just humans at the hospital, no biggie, and the werewolves needed to be taught a lesson."

Jaze dropped all pretense of friendliness. His hands clenched into fists and he took a step forward. Growls emanated from several of the werewolves already in wolf form. He ignored them. "Humans have as much right to live in peace and safety as werewolves do. You've violated every peace treaty we've established between humans and werewolves. As such, you will be marked with trackers and forced to leave this territory. Any action you take to return to an area populated with either werewolves or humans will be met with severe consequences. Do you understand?"

Terence's lips lifted to show his teeth. "I understand you only came with four werewolves." He looked at me and his eyes narrowed. "Make that three and a half. You're outnumbered."

Jaze lowered his head and his eyes shone gold in the starlight. "Try us."

The werewolves rushed forward. Kaynan pulled the blade

from his armband and met two already in wolf form. One charged at Jet and he turned, using the werewolf's momentum to dump him on the ground in a move I recognized very well. A werewolf in wolf form jumped at him when his back was turn. He rolled with the force of the blow and flowed back to his feet in a movement both deadly and graceful; he turned to face the surprised werewolf and his dark eyes narrowed.

I wanted to help them, but the way they fought against the wild pack told of many such occasions together. It was obvious by the careful way they handled the pack that they were trying to defeat them without causing serious injury. I leaned against a pine tree and allowed my exhausted body to relax, watching warily in case I was needed.

Jaze grappled with the leader. Terence slugged him in the stomach, but Jaze breathed with the blow and answered with a jab to the face that bloodied the werewolf's nose. Jaze then hit Terence in the stomach so hard the werewolf staggered backwards. Jaze spun and kicked, catching Terence on the side of the face. The werewolf turned a full circle and fell to his knees.

Two yelps came from Kaynan's wolves; they limped away from him toward the trees. He let them go and watched Jet take down another werewolf.

Something glinted in the starlight. My heart slowed at the sight of a pistol barrel. One of the female werewolves pointed it at Jaze. He didn't notice as he pulled a small object from his pocket and held it to Terence's wrist.

"Jaze, look out!" I shouted just as a black blur dove at the armed werewolf. They went down hard. A low growl emanated from the black wolf as the female struggled to free the gun that was trapped between them. A shot sounded and everyone froze.

HUNTER

"Jet!" Jaze shouted. He left Terence and ran across the camp. Relief showed stark on his face when the black wolf stepped away from the girl.

My heart slowed at the sight of a red pool spreading across the female werewolf's dirty beige shirt.

"Trella!" Terence said in a strangled gasp. No one stopped him when he fell to his knees beside the girl and gathered her in his arms. Tears streaked his cheeks. "Trella, no. Stay with me."

My heart ached. She was already gone. The bullet had fired up under her ribcage, ending her life before she felt the pain. I didn't realize I had crossed the clearing toward them until I stopped a few feet away. Jaze set a hand on Terence's shoulder, regret and sorrow heavy on his face. "I'm sorry," he said quietly. "We never intended for anyone to get hurt."

Terence turned a look of such fierce hatred on the werewolf that Jaze took his hand away. "This is your fault," Terence growled. The vehemence and rage in his voice darkened it to a low rasp. His fiery gaze turned on me. "And yours. You will pay for this."

Jaze's tone was steady when he said, "Terence, Trella's death was an accident."

"Don't say her name!" Terence said, spittle flying from his lips. "You are not worthy to say her name." He gathered her up in his arms and stumbled to his feet.

"Terence, wait," Jaze protested, holding up his hands. "She deserves a proper burial and her family should know what happened."

"Family?" Terence spit in disbelief. "Do you think we'd be out here if we had family? We take care of each other," he concluded. He looked down at the still form in his arms and pain filled his eyes. A wordless roar tore from his lips and he ran out of the camp. The others followed, some limping and others with tears in their eyes.

Silence filled the space beneath the trees. The scent of refuse, rotten pizza, and half-finished beer tangled around us. Jet stood near Jaze's side. There was something in the black wolf's gaze that tore at my heart, a look of regret from one who looked like he didn't regret much.

Jaze rubbed his eyes. "That's not how it was supposed to go."

Kaynan put a hand on his shoulder. "We didn't expect a gun."

Jaze met his gaze, his expression bare. "We should have." He looked around the camp, but it was only a pile of garbage and ratty blankets left as a reminder of what had happened. "Let's go."

"We didn't tag them," Kaynan said quietly.

Jaze let out a breath. "I tagged Terence. They all seem to follow him. We can monitor their movements through him until we can finish tagging the rest of them."

He walked past me, his gaze distant. I fell in next to Kaynan while Jet stalked the trees in wolf form. His black shadow was intimidating and soundless as he ghosted through the fence and across the field.

Kaynan stepped on the lower barbed wire and lifted the upper wires so I could ease through the fence. "Thanks," I said quietly. I followed him across the moon-bathed field feeling more exhausted than I had ever been before. The moonlight on my shoulders gave me the strength to put one foot in front of the other.

"There's something healing about moonlight," Kaynan said, reading my expression.

I glanced at the red-eyed werewolf. He shrugged self-consciously. "I wasn't born a werewolf, but from what I've experienced, I always heal quicker at night when there's a strong moon."

His words surprised me. "You weren't born a werewolf?"

He shook his head. "I was an idiot teenager who made a bad decision that cost me and my sister our lives." He kicked a clump of barley. "A scientist trying to clone werewolves brought us back by mixing our DNA with a werewolf."

That explained his strange eyes and the unusual chemical odor mixed with his scent. Gem would be proud that I was starting to use my nose. I pushed the thought away. The heaviness with which he told his story said there was a lot more he was leaving out. I had kept my own secret for so long I had a strong understanding of the need for privacy. "You must be right. I definitely feel stronger than I did under the trees."

He gave me a grateful smile and nodded. "It's a strange phenomenon."

Both of us avoided talking about what we had seen. I had just watched a girl die. My thoughts were clouded and numb with shock. I realized Kaynan was talking to distract me from the heaviness of the situation.

"How'd you grow up out here?" he asked, looking around at the stretch of fields dotted with hay bales. "I would've gone crazy with nothing to do."

"There's plenty to do," I replied. "Farming keeps you busy enough that you don't know what you're missing." The faint, familiar longing to see new places and experience new things surfaced in my chest. I ignored it. "Life's simple, or at least it was until the wild pack showed up."

We both fell silent until we reached my house. Gem was waiting up for us in the living room. "Vance said you were on your way back," she said, hurrying over to me. She slowed at the looks on our faces. "Is everything alright?"

Jaze shook his head. "Things didn't go as planned, but

they won't be bothering you again."

She nodded and didn't press us with questions.

"If you don't mind, we'll crash here and take off in the morning," Jaze said.

I nodded. "Of course. You guys can have my room."

The door to Mom and Dad's room opened and Mom came down the hall in a robe. "Is everything alright?" she asked. She looked from me to the others. A frown of worry touched her face at their roughed-up appearances.

"Everything's fine," Jaze reassured her. "We've taken care of your problems with the wild pack."

Mom looked at me. I held up my hands. "I didn't fight, honest. I was just showing them to my room."

"I'll grab some sleeping bags and extra blankets," Mom said, making her way to the closet.

I took a seat gingerly in the armchair. Gem snuggled against me and even though it hurt, it was worth it to have her near. I lifted my arm and she settled against my chest. I must have dozed off, because a footstep sounded and I jerked awake to see Mom quietly carrying an armful of wood to the stove. She added the logs, then glanced over and saw that I was awake.

"You both needed the rest," she whispered. "Gem's parents are sleeping well, and Jaze is keeping watch while the others rest. Sleep if you can." I nodded gratefully and she settled a blanket around us before turning to leave the room.

"Mom?" I called softly.

She turned, her gaze questioning.

"Thank you for everything," I said. It fell far short of what I wanted to say, but I couldn't express how much I owed them, how wonderful they had been to me and how understanding. I loved them so much and I had never been one to express it enough. "I love you."

She came over and set a hand gently on my hair, then kissed my forehead. "I love you, too, Dray dear. You'll always be my little boy."

"I know," I said with a smile.

She tucked the blanket carefully around us, then went into the kitchen. I pulled the ottoman close with my feet and stretched out. Gem slept against my side, so small and fragile, yet so strong in her own way. Her pink hair brushed my cheek and I kissed the top of her head. Weariness pulled my eyelids shut; I drifted off in a darkness touched along the edges with fire and the growls of angry wolves.

Chapter 12

When I awoke, the clock on the mantle showed it was just after two in the morning. I closed my eyes again, but sleep eluded me. I eased my arm from beneath Gem's head and left her curled on the armchair snuggled under the blanket. Jo greeted me happily in the kitchen. I grabbed a roll and tossed him a bite, then made my way outside. The puppy gamboled around my feet, then took off across the lawn turned gray by starlight.

My heart slowed at the sight of a form lying on the grass; a breeze told me it was Jaze.

"Couldn't sleep?" he asked quietly. His eyes were on the moon that showed just above the aspens at the edge of our property. The stars glittered down from above, basking the grass and trees in a silvery light that reflected in his gaze.

I shook my head and eased gingerly down on the grass near him. "What are you doing out here?"

Jaze glanced at me. "The moonlight centers my thoughts. Today was a bit," he paused, then concluded, "Trying."

I nodded with the realization that I felt calmer. My thoughts were less scattered and the aches from our fight were fading under the moon's gentle blush. "What is it about the moon?" I asked.

A hint of a smile touched Jaze's face. "I'm not sure, but any werewolf I've talk to has felt the same connection. For me, the moon is a constant in a world that's always changing."

I stared at the night sky, studying the moon and the craters that hollowed its face. A familiar shudder ran down my spine; I suppressed the urge to phase. "I used to be afraid of the moon."

Jaze kept his eyes on the black velvet sky, but

understanding showed in his expression. He let out a slow breath. His presence was comforting in a way I hadn't experienced before. I didn't know if it was because he was an Alpha, or because he had helped me drive the wild werewolves from Thistle, but I felt sure of myself around him, like I knew exactly where I stood. I trusted him.

"What was it about the moon that made you afraid?" he asked quietly.

I frowned and studied the three stars just below the bright orb. They winked lazily as if they held a secret. "When I realized that I changed, phased, whenever the moon was full, I used to dread it. I couldn't hide from its power, no matter what I did, and I couldn't fight it." I spoke quieter, "I guess I feared that anything could have so much control over me."

"The moon isn't so much in control as it is a guide." Jaze spoke the words softly, his tone one of somebody who had never voiced what he told me. He tipped his head to look at me. "What if our phasing is inevitable, but the moon is brightest during our phase to guide our way when it happens so that we aren't completely lost."

My breath caught in my throat. The look in his eyes said that he knew exactly what it felt like to be lost and alone, to feel completely apart from the rest of the world.

"It's nice out here," he said quietly. "I haven't spent much time in the country, but I can definitely feel the appeal of it."

I smiled. "It's pretty peaceful as long as you don't mind the occasional hospital fire or wild werewolf pack."

A shadow crossed Jaze's eyes. "Their presence was all my fault, Dray."

Confused, I asked, "How is that possible? You're just one werewolf."

Surprise touched his gaze. "You're not in awe of having

the great Jaze Carso lying on the grass next to you?" The self-deprecation in his voice made the words ironic instead of boastful.

I fought back a smile. "Until the Hawthornes showed up, I'd never heard of you, but I'm just a simple farm boy."

Jaze watched me with a hint of his own smile. "Somehow I don't think there's anything simple about you."

I let out a breath. "All I want to do is fit in."

He nodded. "Understandable. It was pretty easy appearing normal until other werewolves showed up, right?"

I hesitated, then shook my head. "It wasn't easy at all." I closed my eyes and shut out the world. "All I want to do is play football, stop lying to my friends, and stop failing tests I can pass." The admission surprised me and I glanced at him.

He kept his eyes on the sky. "You fail tests to appear normal?" He fought back a smile, but I could see it in his eyes.

I sighed. "I used to be a straight A student. Homework was easy and I never had to study; then they wanted me take tests to see if I should graduate early."

"So you failed them," Jaze guessed.

"I passed them with low enough marks that I wouldn't make the program. Failing completely would have clued them in that I was marking wrong answers on purpose," I admitted.

A half-smile touched Jaze's lips. "Showing yet again that you're smarter than the system."

I chuckled. "I guess so." We fell silent. The moonlight stretched through the aspens. I swore there was almost an audible hum of life as the grass and bushes were bathed in the captivating light. "What did you mean by it's all your fault?" I asked.

Jaze didn't look at me. I thought for a moment he

wouldn't answer, but he blew out a breath and said, "The fact that there aren't more werewolves, especially other Alphas."

It was my turn to be surprised. "Why would that be your fault?"

Something dark and haunted swept through his dark brown eyes. "My uncle killed my father."

A chill ran down my spine at the look on his face. For a second I saw a child struck by a tragedy so vicious and violent it was still raw in his memories.

He rubbed his eyes with one hand, but no tears showed in them, only unwilling acceptance. "He murdered my father in the midst of his efforts to wipe out all Alphas so he could take over." He glanced at me. "My uncle wasn't an Alpha, and always begrudged my father's position in the pack. Somehow he got it in his mind that if he killed the Alphas, the other werewolves would have to listen to him."

My encounters with Jaze and the other Alphas had given me a great respect for their commanding presence. What little I knew of werewolf hierarchy made me realize that our instincts forced us to obey leadership, something I was still struggling with. "It would work," I realized. An icy dagger ran through my stomach at the realization.

Jaze nodded. "It almost did." Sorrow reflected the moonlight in his eyes; he rubbed them with one hand. Jaze wasn't the type to show weakness. He hid any pain he felt from the blows he had received fighting Terence, and everything about him exuded confident and strength, a leader I would follow. To see him so broken and humble caught at my heart.

"Hundreds of werewolf families went through the same things I did because it took me so long to stop him." His voice choked off, then he said as if he couldn't hold it back, "My mother and I came home to find my father beheaded and quartered. Blood was everywhere. My mother fainted, so I carried her to the car. I gathered up what I could find of him." He fell silent, then he continued, his voice thick with emotion, "I couldn't find his head. I searched our home, but they had taken it." A tear slid slowly down the side of his face and was lost among the grass.

He let out a loud breath. "I lit our house on fire and burned his body inside. When we drove away, I could see the flames in the rearview mirror. I watched my entire life burn."

I didn't know what to say. His eyes were closed, and something about him filled me with deep sorrow. I realized that I could smell his heartache. It was the first time I knew that emotions had a scent.

I shook my head. "I don't know what I would have done. Even though I was adopted, I feel like my parents are mine to protect."

"I know," he whispered.

I rubbed my aching chest. "My biggest fear is that me being a werewolf will somehow affect them. I don't want them hurt." The thought of my parents going through what Gem's had burned through my limbs. The guilt I felt about what had happened with the wild werewolf pack lessened.

"I won't let them get hurt," Jaze said, his voice stronger.

I stared at him. He didn't look at me, but the raw honesty in his voice couldn't be argued against. It if was up to him, my parents would be safe.

I swallowed. "What your uncle did was not your fault."

Jaze turned to look at me. "I should have known."

I shook my head. "You're a high school student. I know I'm not thinking about protecting my parents from merciless killers." My voice dropped. "At least, I wasn't."

Jaze fell silent. He turned his head to watch the fingers of moon shadows that stretched across the grass toward us.

"I've dedicated my life to repairing the damage my uncle did. He killed so many Alphas and hurt so many families. These wild werewolves are one pack of hundreds that we've found, not to mention werewolf fighting rings like the one Jet came from, torture facilities intent on creating more manageable werewolves, which is how Kaynan came to be a werewolf, and armed Hunters who were intent on wiping us from the face of the earth before we created an alliance." He studied the stars as if seeing something else there. "Sometimes it gets overwhelming."

I couldn't imagine everything he held on his shoulders. Suddenly my problems seemed petty and small. I saw school, football, and my friends in a different light. Life in Thistle wasn't bad. In fact, it was close to perfect now that Gem was here and I wasn't alone.

A howl sounded in the distance. An urge to answer the call ran through my veins. "I didn't know there were wolves out here," I said. Other howls rose to mingle with the first, creating a haunting melody that carried over the farmland.

Jaze listened to the voices, then said quietly, "Those aren't wolves; they're werewolves." His forehead creased and his eyes became damp. "They're mourning the loss of the girl from their pack, Trella."

The sorrow in the voices tore at my heart. I had never before understood the way the tones of a howl could convey feelings, but the heartache and loss that colored the night sky wrapped my thoughts in a whisper of their agony.

"I failed them," Jaze said.

I glanced at him and saw that his eyes were closed. "It's not your fault."

He took a breath and let it out slowly. "I should have handled it differently."

"You didn't know they had a gun. Jet could be dead just

as easily as the girl."

Jaze rubbed his eyes. "I know." He looked at me. "I've never had that happen. We've lost werewolves and Hunters freeing other werewolves from horrible situations, but there's never been such a needless waste of life." His voice tightened. "She was Terence's mate. I couldn't imagine losing Nikki."

The thought of losing Gem circled my heart in a fist and made it hard to breathe. I didn't know how deeply I had fallen for her until I thought about losing her. I asked the obvious to chase away the pain of my own thoughts. "You miss her?"

Jaze sat up, his eyes on the dark horizon where the howls faded away. "More than words can express. I'm only half of myself when I'm without her; I feel so incomplete when she's not at my side." He glanced at me. "I've seen the way you and Gem look at each other. I think you understand."

I sat up as well and nodded. "Now that she's in my life, I can't imagine being without her." I thought of Terence and sharp regret filled me. "There's nothing we can do to help him, is there?"

Jaze shook his head. "I just hope he doesn't do anything rash. I don't want any more of his pack to get hurt."

"You said there were a lot more packs like theirs since the Alphas got killed?"

He nodded. "Most of them do fairly well, but some are dangerous like Terence's pack. It takes a lot of work to keep everyone safe."

"I'd like to help," I said quietly. The words surprised me.

Jaze sat back and looked at me, really studied me as if contemplating where I could fit in. A smile hinted around his mouth and his gaze was less harsh as though our conversation had eased some of the tension he carried. "We have a place for you."

HUNTER

I didn't know whether to feel relieved or worried at the thought of leaving my home.

Jaze's next words took that away. "Do what you need to here. You have a good life," he glanced toward the house pointedly, "Loving parents, a wonderful girl, and great opportunities." He met my eyes again, "But if things don't work out in Thistle, we have a place for you."

I suddenly felt lighter, like I had been carrying a weight I didn't notice until it was gone. I held out my hand and Jaze shook it. "Thanks, man," I said.

"Thank you," he said sincerely. The depths to his tone carried far more than the words. Somehow our conversation had helped him. If anything I said eased his burdens at all, I was glad to have helped.

The screen door opened behind us. Kaynan, Vance, and Jet came out. "Thought we'd find you out here," Kaynan said. "You have a thing for grass."

Jaze laughed. "That sounds a lot worse than it is."

Vance stretched out on the lawn next to us. "Can't say you have it wrong. There's something relaxing about it." His eyebrows rose. "Of course, nothing beats the red rocks and warm sand of Two."

Kaynan snorted and lay down as well. "You're crazy," he said. "Give me grass and trees above dirt any day."

"It's not just dirt," the big werewolf argued. "It's sand so fine it feels like powder and smells like cinnamon."

"Oh, cinnamon," Kaynan teased. "Someone's been out in the desert too long."

Both werewolves laughed. I settled back on the grass and heard Jaze do the same. "Come on, Jet," Jaze said. "Even you could use a little relaxation once in a while."

Kaynan shook his head. "You know Jet can't relax. He doesn't have a chill bone in his body."

I kept silent. I couldn't imagine teasing the silent, dark-eyed werewolf who held himself as though ready for an attack at any moment.

"I bet you could do it if you put your mind to it," Vance said, trying and failing to keep the humor from his voice. "You might actually enjoy it."

I heard a slight breath from Jet before he sat down a few feet away.

"Whoa," Kaynan said. "The great warrior sits. Now I've seen it all."

"Lay off him," Jaze answered with a chuckle. "As I recall, his vigilance saved your hide a time or two."

"Or twenty," Jet muttered under his breath.

Everyone burst out laughing.

A comfortable silence fell over the group. The grass was cool and released a scent of green growth and the memory of the noonday sun. Gray brushed the distant edge of the horizon. I felt content lying on the lawn with four other werewolves, our pasts so different, yet with the same goal of living happy, peaceful lives with our loved ones.

"My dad used to take us camping," Kaynan said. Everyone was silent at the red-eyed werewolf's admission. He let out a breath. "We used to look up at the stars like this. Colleen and Dad were into astrology. They knew all the constellations and everything." He took a deep breath. "But before we were werewolves, the grass smelled like just grass, and the breeze was nothing more than a bit of wind, not a messenger carrying scents of the barnyard, livestock, the aspens, the little brook near the edge of the trees, and all of you." He rose up on one elbow. "Baths couldn't hurt, you know."

Jaze chuckled, then said in a serious, quiet voice, "Which way is better."

Kaynan regarded him thoughtfully. "The werewolf or the human?" At Jaze's nod, his gaze drifted to the aspens. "If I could go back to that night and start over before the accident, I probably would have." He took in a breath, then let it out slowly, "But now, no. It's harder for sure, but I love Grace. I couldn't imagine life without her, and I know Colleen is happy with Rafe." A smile touched his lips. "And you guys aren't so bad, either."

He picked a handful of grass and tossed it in the air. The blades caught in the breeze and turned in the fading starlight before they fell. The fresh scent of growth and rain, strength and sunshine touched my nose.

"What about you, Vance?" Jaze asked. "Would you give up what happened at Lobotraz and stay at Two?"

The big werewolf snorted. "I'd probably be stuck there forever if my mother had her way," he said with a chuckle. He pursed his lips and stared at the few stars that still flickered in the waning canopy. "It was the hardest experience of my life," he said in a low voice, his gaze distant. "I almost didn't make it, and I never want any werewolf to go through what I did." He ran a hand unconsciously over the black whip scars on one arm. "But I learned a lot about myself there, and I made it back to Nora." He glanced at me. "Your girl pulled me through, Dray. You need to take care of her."

I nodded, touched by the emotion that thickened his voice. "I will," I said.

He studied me for a few seconds in silence, his gaze hard and calculating. I looked away self-consciously, unable to meet the direct stare of an Alpha. It was a strange feeling knowing that he could best me in strength if he chose. Before I could get too worried, though, he reached over with a beefy hand and slapped me on the shoulder with a laugh. "I know you will. I'm just giving you a hard time."

"As if he hasn't been through enough in the past few days," Jaze said with a chuckle.

I settled back on the grass and felt the last touch of moonlight as the sun chased its silent force from the sky. My aches from the fights surfaced slowly, reminding me of what the moonlight had kept at bay.

"The moon kept me alive," Jet spoke quietly. Shock resonated from the group; they were obviously unaccustomed to such an admission from their silent, deadly member. He didn't look at anyone. His dark gaze was inward, searching something none of us could see. "The moon was the only hope I had, the only gentle thing in my world." He fell silent for a moment, then said, "For most of my life, the moon was my only family, my only friend, the only thing that cared whether I lived or died." His voice carried a depth of pain the likes of which I had never heard before. He pushed his hair back from his eyes and concluded, "I never knew friendship like this could exist. Thank you."

Everyone was looking at him, but he kept his gaze on the moon that stood small and alone in the lightening sky. I realized his thank you had been directed at the moon, not at the werewolves around me. A knot tightened in my throat. Jaze sat up and put a hand on Jet's shoulder. Jet met his eyes. Jaze smiled and Jet gave a short nod in reply. Jaze settled back on the grass. A few seconds later, Jet did as well.

The peace that surrounded us lay thick and comforting, like a blanket that held out the cares each werewolf carried. I felt like I had been given unspoken acceptance into their world, a world where werewolves rescued those who were hurt or in danger, and where families fought to stay together and protect each other against the dangers of a world in which most of the inhabitants were unaware of their secret. They were a group of friends brought together by trials and pain that had hardened and shaped them into the heroes of their race. I felt honored to be with them.

I sat up and counted them aloud. "One, two, three, four, five. Yep, it would work."

"What would?" Jaze asked curiously.

I grinned. "I think you should all quit the rescuing werewolves thing and we could do something that's actually important, like start a basketball team."

Kaynan snorted. "Could you see Vance in a uniform?"

Vance gave a loud laugh. "It wouldn't be hard to find a mascot."

"We'd make one heck of a basketball team," Jaze mused in a serious tone. We stared at him and he cracked a smile. "It wouldn't hurt to keep our options open."

Everyone laughed. Even Jet chuckled at the thought of five werewolves taking on the world through basketball.

"Where'd you find this guy, Jaze?" Vance asked.

"Milking cows on the farm," Jaze replied; everyone laughed again.

"Keep an eye on him," Kaynan said with a chuckle. "Something about him makes big tough werewolves spill their guts like sissies."

"I thought you were a sissy," Vance replied.

Kaynan punched him in the shoulder.

A scent touched my nose and I smiled. "Smells like Mom's making her famous flapjacks." At the others' looks, I laughed. "I guess you'd call them pancakes." I rose to my feet and held out a hand to Jaze.

He smiled and took it. "I can't turn down pancakes."

"Sounds good to me," Vance said, joining us.

Kaynan rose and stretched. "Where's Jet?" he asked, looking around.

Jet was gone. He had disappeared without a sound.

"We'd better get to the kitchen or Jet'll eat all the pancakes without us," Jaze said with a laugh.

Jo met us at the door and followed us into the kitchen. I laughed at the sight of Jet already leaning in the doorway as Mom dished up the first batch of flapjacks. He shot me a weird look and I attempted to turn the laugh into a cough, but failed miserably. Jaze chuckled beside me.

"Fresh flapjacks," Mom said, smiling when she saw us.

We sat at the table and I opened a jar of Mom's raspberry preserves to spread on my flapjacks. I felt a tingle on the back of my neck and looked up to find Jet watching me from across the table. "Want some jam?"

"On pancakes?" he asked the question reluctantly as though he would prefer not to speak at all.

Instincts warned me to leave him alone, but I ignored them. "They're better this way. You spread them with jam, then top them off with maple syrup." At his guarded look, I smiled. "Trust me."

Jaze watched our exchange with great interest. Jet glanced at him and he shrugged. "I'd trust the farm boy," he said.

Jet put down the syrup he had been about to pour over five flapjacks and reluctantly accepted the preserves I held out.

"Do you want a knife?" I asked, holding out my butter knife to him.

Something close to a smile showed in his eyes. "What good's a butter knife?" he asked.

Jaze burst out laughing at some sort of private joke they had. Jet accepted the butter knife and spread jam on top of his pancakes, then he proceeded to dump about half of the syrup container on top. Even Mom watched as he shoveled a bite into his mouth. His eyes lit up and he nodded at me. "It's good," he said in surprise.

HUNTER

I laughed along with Jaze. "Mom canned them herself. Raspberry preserves go with everything."

He quickly ate what was left on his plate. Vance and Kaynan finished close behind. Mom was carrying over the six flapjacks from the next batch and Jet held up his plate.

"Save some for us!" Vance exclaimed.

"Eat your cinnamon dirt," Jet replied.

Vance laughed so hard he choked on a piece of pancake.

Mom laughed and distributed the pancakes the best she could, then went back to cook more.

"At this rate, we'll get one out of every batch if we're lucky," Jaze said to me with a grin. Jet was focused on spreading more preserves over his pancakes and pretended not to hear.

The scent of strawberry and vanilla made my heart race. I turned to see Gem standing in the doorway. Everyone looked up. "Good morning," she said with a shy smile at our sudden attention.

"I saved you a seat," I said, patting the one next to me. I lifted the platter on top to reveal three warm flapjacks. "And I managed to hide a few pancakes from Jet."

He stared at me and I laughed at the disbelief on his face. "I have a few tricks up my sleeve," I said.

His eyes narrowed slightly, but there was the barest hint of a smile on his face. "I'm keeping an eye on you, farm boy."

Jaze laughed so hard he dropped his fork and it clattered to the floor. He picked it up and wiped it off with his napkin. "I think Thistle's been good for this group," he said.

Gem took the seat next to me. "I'm glad to see everyone is in such good spirits," she said with her pixie smile.

I nodded. "How are your parents?"

"Better," she said. She and Mom exchanged a smile. "Much better, thanks to you and your family."

"We're happy to help," I replied.

"And you are welcome to stay as long as you'd like," Mom said. "I've called a few ladies and we'll be working to right the damage to your house."

Tears glittered in Gem's eyes. "You don't have to do that."

Mom patted her arm. "Nonsense, honey. We neighbors have to take care of each other," she said with a wink.

Gem looked at me and I nodded. "It's the country life," I said.

She leaned against me and I breathed in the scent of her freshly washed hair.

I heard Dad's footsteps in the mudroom and smiled when he came into the kitchen. "What's for breakfast?" he asked.

"Apparently not enough," Mom replied. We all started laughing.

HUNTER

Chapter 13

I stared in amazement at the jet that sat in the middle of Thistle's miniature airport. Only two crop dusters and a small two-person plane occupied the side of the tarmac.

Gem gave Vance a tight hug. "Thanks for coming out, you guys," she said.

"Keep an eye on that boy," Vance said with a nod in my direction. "He's alright."

"He is," Gem replied. She threw me a smile.

"Take care of yourself," Jaze said. He held out a hand and I shook it.

"You, too," I replied.

He nodded. "You've given me a few things to think about."

Kaynan and Vance followed Jaze inside. Jet was about to join them when my mom pulled something from her purse and handed it to him. He accepted the jar of raspberry preserves with a surprised expression.

"Like Dray said, it's good on just about anything," she told him.

Jet gave a full smile this time. "I'll test that theory."

She pointed to the jar. "I wrote our number on it. Call me when you're out and we'll send you some more. There's no shortage of preserves at our house."

He nodded with an embarrassed smile and disappeared into the jet. A few minutes later, I was surprised to see Jaze pull on a headset and perform the starting procedures.

"Those kids keep surprising me," Dad said with a shake of his head.

Gem slipped her hand into mine. "We owe them a great deal," she said.

I thought of Jaze's words and the burden he carried on

his shoulders. "I think he's just happy to help," I replied. She nodded and we walked together back to the car.

We found Gem's parents waiting in the living room. "We wanted to thank you for your hospitality," Anna said, her eyes bright. "You've been so kind to open your house to us." She swallowed and blinked quickly, "And for cleaning our home."

"It was our pleasure," Mom replied. She and Anna hugged. "You call us if you need anything at all."

"We will," Anna promised.

Greg and Dad shook hands in the hearty, silent way men express their appreciation. Greg then turned to me. "Dray, that was a brave thing going after that pack."

I dropped my eyes, my heart heavy. "I shouldn't have thought I could ask them to leave town. It was foolish and you both were hurt because of it."

Greg put a hand on my shoulder. "Don't hold that guilt. Those werewolves were trouble. They proved it with their actions at the hospital. Thistle is better off without them."

I nodded and he tightened his hold. "You're a good kid, Dray. I'm glad Gem found you."

"Me, too," I said, glancing at her. A smile spread across my face as she grinned at both of us, her feet shuffling as if she was so excited to go home she couldn't hold still.

When her dad let go of my shoulder, she held out her hand. "See you tomorrow, Dray."

I laughed and shook it. "See ya, Gem."

She led the way out the door to her parents' car I had helped drive over. Her parents walked arm in arm gingerly down the porch steps. Jo pranced around their feet, but was careful not to trip them. I used to be amazed at the dog's canny ability to sense when someone was hurt. Now I understood that it, too, was a scent, the scent of blood, healing wounds, and the exhaustion that such healing carries.

HUNTER

I gave off that scent as well, as much as I hated to admit it. Jo hovered at my feet when they left. I patted his head, touched by the puppy's concern.

***

I stayed at home an extra day to catch up on sleep and recuperate. Dad took care of the farm and wouldn't let me help him even when I told him I was going crazy indoors. "Train Jo to do something useful," he replied with a slight smile.

I took him up on it and had the puppy sitting, staying, and rolling over by the end of the day, much to Mom's delight.

By the time I walked with Gem to school the next day, I was so ready for a change of atmosphere I was actually excited to sit through class. I didn't mind the quiet buzz at school about the hospital, and wrote off my few remaining bruises as having occurred during the fire, which increased the commotion.

I was finally beginning to relax when the intercom rang during Algebra and a strange voice called over the intercom, "Please send Dray Dawson to the office."

I figured it was the Principal trying for another shot at the medal, but when I walked up the hall I saw Gem standing anxiously by the front doors, her finger entwined and her eyes on a car out front. She stepped from foot to foot as though she wanted to be anywhere else than there.

"Gem, what's going on?"

She turned at my voice and ran down the hall. She caught my hand, her eyes worried. "I don't know. They won't tell me anything except we need to go with the government official in Principal McCormick's office."

I glanced at the front desk. "They're not allowed to release us to anyone but our parents." Ms. Crenshaw watched us curiously and gave me a cheerful smile when she met my eyes.

"They have a letter from our parents." Her tone increased

my worry. She looked at me seriously. "I just spoke to my mom on the phone. She says we need to go with them and they'll explain everything to us in the car."

A man in a dark blue suit with a red handkerchief in his pocket came out of the office with Principal McCormick at his side. The Principal spotted us and walked over. "It sounds like news of your valor has gotten out despite your efforts, Mr. Dawson," the Principal said with a kind smile. "You're going to get the recognition you deserve." He turned to Gem. "And I had no idea of your part in it, Ms. Hawthorne. I'm grateful we have such brave students in our midst."

"As am I," the man in the suit said. His smile looked forced, but instinct told me to return it.

"It's not necessary," I replied carefully, "But thank you."

"We have a letter from both of your parents releasing you into Agent Sullivan's care. Enjoy your time with him. You deserve what you get."

A pit formed in my stomach at the Principal's words, but he smiled with innocent cheer and waved us on our way.

Gem and I followed the agent into the waiting limo. The excitement of being in a limousine for the first time was overshadowed by the heavy silence of our suited companion. Gem and I took the seat facing the back of the car, a strange experience which reminded me of riding in the back of a truck, but lacked the open air and the simple freedom of being able to jump off if you wanted. The driver, a man hidden behind the tinted separation window, pulled out of the parking lot. The hum of the wheels sounded loud in the palpable silence.

Agent Sullivan cleared his throat. "Introductions are in order. I am Agent Sullivan of the Global Protection Agency." He paused and when we didn't say anything, he continued, "I've assisted with several other werewolf-related missions, specifically with Kaynan and Colleen Anderson."

I felt Gem tense beside me. "What about them?" I asked, trepidation rising in my chest.

His green eyes darkened slightly. "We have a situation."

"I figured as much," I replied dryly. I was tired of him beating around the bush when we had no choice but to go along with it.

A slight smile touched his lips. "I apologize for the inconvenience of our situation, but I need to ask for your patience." He looked at each of us in turn. "You had several friends visit you three days ago, am I correct?"

I kept still, but Gem nodded quickly. "Are they alright?"

Agent Sullivan's forehead creased. "We hope so, but we can't be certain."

Gem's face washed pale. "What happened?" She grabbed my hand and a surge of frustration ran through me. After all she had been through, she didn't deserve more worry and the Agent's elusiveness was stressing her out more.

"Get to the point, please." I added the 'please' as an afterthought, figuring Mom's mantra of 'politeness doesn't hurt anyone' probably applied. "The sooner we know what's going on, the better we'll be able to help."

Agent Sullivan nodded. He moved to the edge of his seat and spread his hands. "The jet that Jaze and his friends rode home was waylaid on the tarmac upon landing. Jaze and the three werewolves with him were taken."

Gem gasped and her hold on my hand tightened. I tried to stay calm. "What do we know?"

"That the men who took them aren't employed by a government agency for any nation. Instead, they are renegades, mercenaries for the highest bidder. Our assumption is that they're going to sell Jaze."

My mouth fell open as I tried to think it through. "Why

go through so much trouble to sell one werewolf?"

Agent Sullivan gave me a frank look. "How well do you know Jaze, Mr. Dawson?"

I met his gaze. "Enough to consider him a friend."

He nodded and glanced at Gem. "And you, Ms. Hawthorne?"

She took a calming breath and I felt her tremble slightly. "They rescued my friends and I from a werewolf torture facility. I owe him a great deal."

The Agent nodded as if unsurprised to hear it. "Jaze Carso is the nationally recognized leader of the North American werewolves. He is considered the most powerful werewolf as far as connections are concerned."

Something Vance had said two nights before came to my mind, "He's done so much for the werewolves in this country that if he calls for a favor, everyone's eager to respond," I repeated slowly, "So someone would buy Jaze because if he says jump. . . ."

"Every werewolf and Hunter within hearing would ask how high," Agent Sullivan concluded. "Buy Jaze and they would have every pack at their command." My hands clenched into fists at the thought.

Gem shook her head quickly. "That doesn't make sense. Jaze is the most loyal werewolf I know. He wouldn't put others in danger to save himself."

The Agent's gaze lowered. "It took me two days to come back here because I had to verify my suspicions, but whoever took Jaze wasn't messing around. They took Jaze's girlfriend, Nikki Valen, Nikki's parents, and Jaze's mother, along with the male werewolves he flew with and the female werewolves of his pack." He met my eyes seriously. "I don't know any werewolf or human that could ignore the torture of their own kin. They have enough leverage to ensure his compliance."

My stomach turned over. "What can we do to help?"

The Agent put his hands on his knees. "To be honest, I've been instructed not to be involved in this situation."

I watched him closely. "What do you mean?"

His brow lowered. "My agency has been told to stay out of werewolf matters. Apparently other agencies have interest where they are concerned." His tone was dark and a chill of warning ran down my spine.

"What kind of interest?" I asked.

The Agent gave me a searching look. "I wish I knew," he finally said.

Gem watched us both, her blue eyes wide with worry. "Then why are you here?"

Agent Sullivan tapped his fingers on one knee, then seemed to realize he was doing it and stopped. "I owe Jaze, Kaynan, and Colleen for saving my children. I'm not supposed to be involved, but I'll do anything in my power to see them back home safely."

"As would we," I replied. I stared out the tinted window, my mind racing as I thought of my talk with Jaze in the early hours of the morning. He cared so much for others. After all he had been through, the last thing he deserved was to have those he loved used as fodder to bend him to the will of the highest bidder.

I met his eyes. "Tell us where to go. We'll make sure they get safely home." It was a big promise, but one I intended to keep. Gem nodded next to me.

Agent Sullivan gave a small smile. "I was hoping as much. I can't ensure your protection."

I shrugged. "You weren't here, right?"

The smile touched his eyes. "Right."

HUNTER

Chapter 14

"I think you guys know each other," Agent Sullivan said as he led the way to a jet sitting at Thistle's small airport. Several people watched us from the shack that acted as a control building for the crop dusters. It wasn't every day Thistle had jets land, and there had been two in less than a week. I was mildly surprised the reporter wasn't taking pictures for the Thistle Times.

"Mouse!" Gem cried. She threw her arms around the shoulders of a skinny boy with light brown hair and glasses who waited at the bottom step of the jet. He shoved the glasses up his nose looking uncomfortable and pleased at the same time. "How did you escape?"

"They never found me," Mouse replied in a soft voice. He looked at the floor. "I hid in the attic at my grandma's."

Gem's eyebrows pulled together and she looked him over quickly. "It must have been so hard to see them go and not know where they were being taken."

"I knew," Mouse said. At her surprised look, he gestured to the small laptop he carried. "Kaynan's wristband has a tracking chip. I've been following them for the last three days."

"Why haven't you sent the Hunters and werewolves?" Gem asked.

Mouse's happiness at seeing Gem faded from his eyes. He blinked and kept his eyes on the laptop. "Only a few select leaders of the Hunter/Werewolf Coalition knew that Jaze was going to Thistle."

The implication made me sick. "So someone Jaze trusted betrayed him."

Mouse nodded without looking at me. "I didn't know who we could involve safely, so I contacted Agent Sullivan."

"Where are we going from here?" I asked.

"Agent Sullivan's given me access to his sources. All indications point to a drop off in California. The names of the terrorists who hold Jaze and the others are also linked to a warehouse south of San Francisco. They're moving using cargo boxes on semi-trucks." He shoved his glasses further up his nose. "We have one day before they reach California. Agent Sullivan has found us a facility where we can train. We plan to hit them tomorrow night."

I looked at the Agent. "I thought you couldn't get involved."

He glanced at the jet. "Since Jaze's jet is grounded, Mouse needed transportation and a team. As long as everything follows according to plan, we're in, but I'm pushing my limits here. Anything out of the lines and we're done."

I nodded. "Fair enough."

We climbed into the jet and I watched the ground fade quickly from view. I was leaving my home. It was my first time away from Thistle since my adoption. I wasn't sure if it was the want of a wolf to be home in my territory, or the thought of the danger that lay ahead of us, but my stomach was in knots.

Gem rested her head against my shoulder. Her scent of sunshine and strawberries was mixed with something flat and slightly acidic. Worry, my brain categorized for me. I put my arm around her. She tipped her head up and I kissed her on the nose. She stared at me, her blue eyes wide and a hint of a smile on her lips despite her concern. I pulled her close and her arms wrapped around me.

"They're going to be alright," I whispered.

She nodded but didn't say anything.

HUNTER

***

The warehouse was an empty shell that smelled of sawdust and mice.

"We expect them to hold Jaze and the others just long enough for whatever negotiation or auction they have planned, then he'll be moved again," Agent Sullivan said. "We'll only have a small window in which to act."

The five agents who made up our team listened carefully. They looked unassuming, but when we arrived we had the chance to watch them practice as they swept the warehouse and announced it clean. The four men and one woman worked with the swift efficiency of a flight of birds, always aware of each other's location and using nonverbal communication to sweep together without impeding any of the others' movements.

"We expect him to be held here," Mouse said. He indicated the small room that once served as the warehouse's office. "Thermal imaging from our droid over the other warehouse shows men already waiting there."

Agent Sullivan nodded. "Dray, Gem, you'll act as backup for the team. I don't want you in the heat of the action if we can help it, but I won't expect Jaze's pack to follow anyone out they don't know, especially after all they've been through."

We ran several simulations following strict protocols Agent Sullivan and Mouse set up. I felt secure with the team, and the confidence on Gem's face showed that she agreed. We both carried guns and wore tactical vests, but they were only for worse case scenarios.

We ran one last simulation in which Agent Sullivan's team took out a dozen pretend guards at the door, took out another dozen with stealth kills in the first room, then successfully overpowered five more in the office. Only one

Agent was considered compromised.

Agent Sullivan glanced at his watch. "We have half an hour. Let's get ready."

The team followed him out the door. Gem and I trailed behind. I looked back to see if Mouse was coming, but he was staring at his computer. His glasses sat slightly askew; he didn't appear to notice.

"What's wrong?" I asked, pausing. Gem stopped short, her eyes on Mouse as well.

He looked up, his face pale. "The signal's moved."

"What do you mean?" I demanded. A pit began to form in my stomach.

"They were following major freeways, then the signal stopped and I assumed they were gassing up the trucks, but now it's moving in a north-western direction."

"Which means?" Gem asked.

His eyes met mine. "There aren't any roads where the signal is. They've been moved to a train. They must have realized they've been compromised."

My heart fell. "Where are they headed?"

Mouse shook his head, his eyes moist. "I'm not sure."

"Not sure about what?"

We turned to find Agent Sullivan in the warehouse doorway. Mouse and I exchanged a look. "We're moving outside of the lines," I said.

Agent Sullivan crossed to us and looked at Mouse's computer. He was silent for a full minute, then he let out a breath and shook his head. "I'm sorry, guys; we've got to pull out."

Mouse looked like he was ready to cry. His jaw was clenched and he kept his eyes firmly on the floor, but I saw tears in his eyes and a slight quiver to his lip. My heart went out to the small, brilliant werewolf.

"You have to pull out, but I don't," I said quietly. Gem's fingers threaded through mine and she held my hand tightly.

Agent Sullivan and Mouse looked at me. I met the Agent's gaze. "Get us to the train. I'll take care of the rest."

"We'll take care of the rest," Gem concluded.

His brows pinched together and he watched us worriedly. "I can't guarantee your safety."

"You said that already," I reminded him.

A small smile touched his lips. "I just wanted to make sure you remembered."

***

A helicopter landed near the warehouse a few minutes later. The Agent's team was reluctant to see us go, but they were under orders and knew they had no choice. Gem and I took our seats and pulled on headsets. Agent Sullivan sat in the front next to the pilot.

I studied the landscape below. Trees dotted the ground between fields and expanses of shrubs and dirt used as range for cattle. The thrill I felt at being in a helicopter was tempered by the thought of Jaze and the others in trouble.

Our conversation played over again in my head, the comfort I felt in his presence and the way he talked to me with an honesty and openness that tore down my walls and allowed me to trust him. He carried so much weight on his shoulders taking care of the werewolves, and now somebody had betrayed him to an end more horrible than I wanted to consider.

Gem's hand covered mine. When I looked up, I saw she had taken off her headset; I did the same.

"Are you ready for this?" she asked. The sound of the chopper pounded against my ears, but my werewolf hearing picked up her voice easily within the steady thrum. I nodded. I didn't know what to expect, but action was better than the anticipation that had curdled in my stomach all day. I was happy to be on our way to help Jaze and his pack, even if we didn't know what to expect.

Gem blinked and looked down. My heart turned over at the emotions that filled her eyes. "I'm afraid, Dray." I pulled her close and she leaned against my chest with her head under my chin. "I don't want to go back," she said softly enough that I almost didn't hear her.

Ice ran through my veins at the thought of Gem in a cage again. "We need to take you back." I put on my headset. "We need to turn around," I told the pilot. Agent Sullivan looked back at me. "Gem can't do this. We need to take her home."

"No!" Gem protested.

"If we go back, we'll miss the drop," Agent Sullivan said over the headset.

I looked into her eyes. "Gem, I'm not going to let you go through that again. If there's even a chance that they're going to take you, I won't risk it."

"I need to help Jaze," she said. "I'm going with you."

I shook my head. "It's too dangerous. I promised you that I wouldn't let you get hurt again."

"I'll be alright," she said. Her hand slipped from mine and her blue eyes flashed with passion. "I can take care of myself."

"No, you can't," I shot back, "And I won't be able to protect you."

Agent Sullivan looked back at us. "What's the call?"

"We're freeing Jaze and the others," Gem said without hesitation. She met my eyes, daring me to argue.

The mourning howls from Terence's pack rose in my head. In a flash I saw Gem's lifeless body instead of Trella's; my own mourning cry haunted my thoughts. I gritted my teeth and bit back a response, but wondered if I would regret it for the rest of my life.

Chapter 15

"This is where we part ways," Agent Sullivan said.

We stood on a red rock ledge overlooking a steep valley that was dissected by a single line of train tracks. The unfamiliar weight of my bulletproof vest was a constant reminder of the challenge we faced.

"I'm sending you on a death mission," Agent Sullivan said quietly. "Maybe I shouldn't have gotten you involved." The doubt I heard in the Agent's voice was the first he had shown since we were forced to change plans. His concern for our safety was stark on his face.

I met Gem's eyes. She smiled at me, her own fear at the situation shielded beneath her bravery. Vance was right. She was the strongest person I had ever met.

"We'll do our best," I told him. I held out a hand. "You'd better get going."

He nodded and shook it, then turned the Gem. "I didn't know plans would change," he said apologetically.

"Jaze gave me my life back," she replied. "Maybe I can repay the favor."

Agent Sullivan nodded. "Take care."

We watched him drive away. The sound of a train horn called in the distance. The sun was setting between the mountains, casting the valley in shades of gold.

"Ready?" I asked.

Gem nodded. The only sign she gave of her fear was her tight grip on my hand and the slight crease to her brow. On impulse, I pulled her close and kissed her. My heart thundered and I felt like I held the most precious thing in the world within my arms. Gem gasped in surprise, then her hands wrapped in my hair and she kissed me back. For that moment, we were the only two people in the world.

HUNTER

Her scent surrounded me, and when I stepped back, the taste of her kiss lingered on my lips. I put my forehead against hers. "I love you, Gem Hawthorne."

Her eyes looked up into mine with fierce intensity. The dancing spark that filled them melted my heart. "I love you, Dray Dawson," she whispered.

I pulled her close and she held me with a strength belied by her petite body.

"We're going to make it through this," I said, though the doubt in my words was obvious to both of us. This was a suicide mission and we knew it.

"No matter what happens," Gem said, "I'll always love you."

A smile spread across my face and warmed my soul. "Then everything was worth it.

A grin turned her lips and she slid her hand into mine again. "Let's do this."

I put a hand to my earpiece. "Testing, testing. Come in Mother Wolf, this is Lone Wolf. Do you copy?"

Mouse's voice came over the earpiece, his tone dry. "You can just call me Mouse."

I exchanged a grin with Gem. "Oh, sure. Take all the fun out of it."

Mouse didn't bother to reply.

I looked up but the drone Mouse was using the track the train was merely a black dot against the evening sky. He was still at the warehouse, his computer set up to monitor both the drone and the tracking chip. With his 3D thermal imaging and our ear pieces, he would be our eyes and ears when we were on top of the boxcars.

The train approached our jump-off point. It was a freighter pulling cargo boxcars. Mouse spoke in our earpieces. "The imaging shows seven bodies in the third car and ten in the three following it. The rest of the boxcars are carrying groups of four except for the first and second, which are empty. From the position of the bodies, it looks like boxes three, four, and five are our most likely targets."

"Where do we start?" Gem asked, eyeing the train as it barreled up the tracks.

"Jump on the second, then work your way down. That way they won't hear you coming. If you find Jaze first, great; otherwise, you'll have help getting him out."

Gem's hand tightened in mine. We stepped to the edge of the cliff. It was a good thirty foot drop to the tracks below; our timing had to be perfect.

I counted in my head. The train looked faster than it had before. I told myself it was my imagination. I let out a slow breath. "Ready?" I asked quietly. I saw Gem nod out of the corner of my eye. "Three, two, one, jump," I yelled.

The space between the cliff and the train felt much shorter than it looked. I rolled with the jarring impact of the metal roof and grabbed one of the ribs that lined the top. Gem slid down, her hands scrambling for purchase. I caught her arm. She met my eyes, her own wide with fright as I pulled her up beside me.

"The hard part's over," I said in her ear.

She gave me a smile and rolled her eyes; the wind rushed past, sweeping the sounds of our landing away. We had reached on the second boxcar as planned. I motioned toward the third and she nodded.

I gritted my teeth and jumped the gap between the cars. I turned to help Gem, but she was already beside me. She smiled at my surprise, her short pink hair whipping in the wind. Love for her beat so strongly in my chest I wanted to kiss her again. I forced down the impulse and took her hand. We crossed to the edge of the boxcar.

HUNTER

The only access inside was a single door on the long side of the car. I knelt and grabbed the edge of the door with both hands. Gem did the same. We pulled and the door slid grudgingly to the right. Commotion rose from below. "Wait here," I shouted. She nodded.

I grabbed the edge of the boxcar and swung inside. I blinked at the sudden darkness and my eyes adjusted to wolven grays. My heart slowed at the sight six men standing around a lone figure bound and gagged on the floor. A quick breath told me the prisoner was Jet. Four of the men rushed forward.

I ducked a punch and slammed a fist into one man's stomach, then turned and elbowed another on the side of the head. I blocked a kick and followed with a punch to a man's groin, then kicked another in the chest with my cowboy boot. He staggered back and I followed, using his body to push through the last two so that I could stand over Jet. I blocked a kick and took a punch to the ribs.

I wanted to phase. I had never fought humans as a wolf; of course, I hadn't fought humans in human form, either. Energy thrummed through my limbs, willing me to let go of my control and give in to my wolven instincts. I gritted my teeth against the urge. I told myself over and over that I needed to stay in human form to help the others. I couldn't climb boxcars as a wolf, no matter how much the need to phase called to me.

One man kicked Jet and he stifled a groan. He couldn't see past the blindfold. The scent of blood was heavy in the air. I could only imagine what they had done to him.

I dove at the man and tackled him to the ground. He tried to force himself on top, so I turned with him and used his momentum to throw him out the open door. A club slammed into my back and I fell back to the floor, dazed. I rolled over, just missing a blow that would have done considerable damage to my skull.

I grabbed the club and jerked the man forward, then kicked him in the chin with my boot from where I lay on the floor. His head snapped back and he fell over Jet to land in an unmoving heap on the ground.

When I rose to my feet, the one I had punched in the stomach ran at me like a bull, slamming me into the boxcar wall. I drove both elbows into his back and simultaneously brought a knee up into his stomach. He staggered back several steps toward the open door. I rushed him the way he had me and threw him out into the darkness.

The man I had elbowed in the side of the head leaned unmoving against one wall, one whimpered in pain in the corner, and two more were unconscious near Jet's feet, no longer a threat.

I knelt next to Jet and he struggled to back away. "Jet, it's me, Dray. I'll get you out of here," I said.

"Is he alright?" Mouse asked over the earpiece.

"I think so."

Jet tipped his head toward me and my breath caught in my throat at the sight of blood coating the side of his face beneath the rags tied across his eyes and mouth. I worked quickly at the knots and pulled the cloth free. "Why did they do this to you?" I asked, horrified at his condition.

Jet's dark blue eyes were filled with pain. "I don't make a good prisoner. Where's Jaze?" he croaked out. Blood trickled from the corner of his mouth and a welt bled above his eye. His shirt was soaked in sweat and I could smell fresh blood from other parts of his body. Whoever had kidnapped them wasn't fooling around.

I tried to push my emotions aside. "I'm not sure, but we'll find him. This is the first boxcar we checked." I reached behind Jet and grabbed the thick black chains around his wrists. I bit back a gasp as they burned my hands. A thick substance coated my palms. I wiped them quickly on my pants. "I'm hoping the others are here, too."

"What others?" his words were quiet, but laced with steel.

I hesitated, unsure what I should tell him. He turned his head to face me.

"Tell him," Mouse said.

I took a bracing breath. "They didn't just take you guys. They found Jaze's pack and kidnapped anyone they could use as leverage against him."

Something flashed through Jet's eyes, an emotion I had never seen in them before. I realized it was fear. "Do they have Taye?" he asked.

I didn't recognize her name, but Agent Sullivan wasn't sure how many werewolves they had taken. The look on Jet's face was unmistakable; whoever she was, he loved her. "I'm not sure," I said honestly. I put a hand to the earpiece. "Do you know, Mouse?"

"She's in the train," Mouse replied. "They took everyone."

Jet closed his eyes, an action so unlike his usual silent, dangerous front that my heart went out to him. I touched his shoulder. "We'll find her."

He opened his eyes and the pain and fear were gone. Instead, fierce determination filled them. "Get me out of these chains," he growled.

I looked around, but the boxcar was empty of anything I could use as leverage. I gritted my teeth and grabbed the chains. When I pulled, they didn't budge. My hands burned.

"Men are climbing on top of the boxcars. They know you're here," Mouse said quickly. "Gem needs your help."

A thump sounded on top of the boxcar. I closed my eyes

and thought of the Harrison's car with the train barreling down. I took a steeling breath and pulled harder. The links began to open, first one, then two. Suddenly, the link in the center broke completely.

I dropped the chains and tried to wipe off the grease that coated my hands, but my palms were burned to the point that I could barely stand to touch them. I gingerly helped Jet to his feet. He wavered slightly, then his jaw clenched and he stood straight. "Let's go."

Another thump sounded from above. I ran to the edge of the boxcar and pulled myself back onto the roof in time to see four figures fighting Gem in the rapidly falling darkness. She was about half their size, but she held her own against their onslaught.

Gem blocked a punch and dove under the legs of one, then kicked him in the groin before she jumped back to her feet. Another tried to grab her in a bear hug, but I punched him in the kidney, then slammed a left haymaker into the back of his head. He slumped to the ground.

The last two attacked me at the same time. I rolled with the force of the first one's momentum and threw him over my head and off the train. The second one threw a punch when I rose to my feet, but Jet was there as silent as a shadow. He intercepted the punch and slid around the attacker with the lethal grace of a hunting cat. The man's eyes widened when Jet hit him twice in the stomach and once in the neck. He then ducked under the man's outstretched arm and hit him low in the back. The man's eyes rolled back and Jet lowered him down.

Gem stared at them, her chest heaving. "Are you okay?" I asked in her ear. The wind whistled past us, carrying the scent of desert sagebrush and dirt that dotted the falling darkness. The boxcar rocked under my feet with the steady rhythm of the wheels on the rails.

She nodded and said, "Two of them were werewolves from Thistle."

My blood ran cold. I looked at the two who moaned on the roof. Sure enough, both had been part of our battle outside the town. With the gathering darkness and the wind carrying their scents away, I hadn't recognized them. I didn't have time to think about what it meant.

"Catch up to Jet," Mouse said.

I looked up to see him already crossing to the next car. Three men stood waiting. He attacked them without hesitation.

Gem grabbed my hand. Pain ran from my burned palm, but I ignored it and slipped my fingers through hers. We jumped the gap just as two of Jet's combatants fell to the roof and the third was thrown over the side. I knelt down to slide the door open, but the metal bit into the raw flesh of my palms and I jerked my hands back.

"What happened?" Gem asked. She took one of my hands, then gasped at the sight of melted skin. It would heal, but not until I had the chance to wash them.

"Jet's cuffs were coated in some sort of silver grease. It'll be fine," I said. "But the doors are a bit difficult to manage."

Jet watched me, his expression intense. He didn't say a word, but leaned down and yanked the door to the side and slipped off the roof. The sound of fighting ensued. I debated whether Gem would be safer on top of the train, but the last time I left had her facing four attackers on her own.

"Be careful," I said. She nodded and swung into the boxcar. I gritted my teeth against the pain of the metal and followed.

My feet were swept out from under me the second I hit the floor. I rolled and jumped back to my feet in time to avoid a knife swipe at my stomach. I blocked another lunge and planted a punch square in my attacker's face. His nose crumpled under my fist and blood blossomed across his face as he fell backwards.

I turned in time to see Gem dodge a punch, then kick one of the wild werewolves out the open door. Jet already had two still forms at his feet and fought a third. He blocked a kick with his forearm, punched his attacker in the groin, followed it with a punch to the stomach, another to the throat so quickly I could barely follow his movements, then slipped behind the werewolf and dropped him with a blow to the neck.

He immediately ran to four forms who sat bound and gagged against the far wall. "Wait," I said. He paused and I tossed him a knife from the werewolf who had attacked me and now huddled clutching his nose in the corner.

Gem and I removed blindfolds and gags while Jet used the knife to pry the chains open without touching them.

As soon as the last girl was free, Jet gathered her in his arms. She hugged him back as fiercely. "Are you alright?" he whispered; the concern in his voice was so strong a lump formed in my throat.

She nodded, her blue-gray eyes soft and kind. "Are you?" she asked, touching his bruised cheek gently.

He nodded. "I am now."

I helped the girls to their feet. They looked a little roughed up, but nowhere nearly as bad as Jet. "Have you found Jaze?" a girl with long black hair and blue eyes asked.

"That's Nikki," Mouse said in my earpiece. I was surprised to smell that she was human. A dark purple bruise ran from her cheekbone to her jawline and blood crusted a cut in her lip, but she didn't seem to care.

"We haven't yet, but we will," I reassured her.

"Dray, you need to get going," Mouse said. "A helicopter is on its way, and it's not one of ours."

Jet and Taye stood near a woman with blond hair and kind eyes whom I guessed to be Jaze's mother. "Everything's going to be alright," Jet said. She blinked in the semi-darkness, her concern for her son bright in her gaze.

"Who's helping you?" the woman next to her asked. Her scent told that she was another human.

"Just Dray and Gem," Jet said. "But it's enough."

"And Mouse," Mouse said in my earpiece as I said the words out loud. Everyone looked at me. "Agent Sullivan told us what happened," I explained. "Mouse is helping us from an advantage point, but we don't have much time. A helicopter is on its way."

"Then we'd better hurry," Gem said. She spoke to the women. "Stay here. We'll come back for you."

Taye shook her head. "I'm going with you." She held Jet's hand tight, her expression determined.

Jet shook his head. When she opened her mouth to protest, he pulled her close. "I can't protect Jaze if I'm worried about you." His eyes held hers, pleading for understanding. Jet's fierce façade crumbled in Taye's presence and he became something more human and less fearless warrior. She touched a hand to his cheek and he blinked, his expression bare.

Gem slipped her arm through mine and leaned her head against my shoulder as we watched them. The whole conversation took place in a matter of seconds, but lately, the seconds meant more than an eternity.

"Dray, get on top, now!" Mouse said.

"Take care of yourself," Taye whispered to Jet. Jet nodded and let her go. He crossed to the open door, glanced back once, then pulled himself easily to the top of the train.

Adrenaline ripped through my veins like fire. I grabbed the top of the boxcar and pulled myself up. My raw hands slipped just before I reached the top and I slid, then fingers encircled my wrist and dragged me up. My heart thundered in my chest as I crouched on top of the train. Jet let me go when he was certain I was set. "Look," he commanded.

I followed his gaze. Time slowed. A helicopter flew close to the fifth boxcar on the train, the one I guessed Jaze was in. The thrumming of the blades caught my ears before it was snatched away by the eager wind. Figures moved in the darkness on top of the boxcar hooking up chains to attach to the helicopter.

Jet and I exchanged a glance and we took off running. We leaped the gap between our boxcar and the next, then crossed to the last car without breaking stride. I slammed into the side of a werewolf just as he was attaching the cable to a hook from the helicopter that flew about ten feet overhead. The wind pushed the helicopter from side to side as it fought to keep centered.

Two others tackled me when we hit the ground. I rolled and threw them, then reached my feet just as another werewolf grabbed the hook from the helicopter. I realized he was trying to free it, not attach it to the boxcar for carrying. A warning bell sounded in the back of my mind.

I grabbed the werewolf by the shoulder. He turned and an agonizing fire ran down my arm. I stumbled backwards. A silver blade stuck out of my shoulder just where the bulletproof vest ended. Numbness spread through the right side of my body. I stared at the werewolf.

"Should've given up," Terence spat. "Jaze'll pay for killing Trella."

"It was an accident," I growled. I tried to pull the knife from my shoulder, but it hurt too much to touch it. The boxcar under our feet rocked and I fought to keep my footing.

"They promised me he'd suffer before they killed him," he said with a toothy grin. He moved to unhook the helicopter again, but I rushed at him. He stumbled on one of the ribs that crossed the top of the boxcar and fell backward. I tackled him and he kicked, trying to send me off the train. I held onto the ribs and pulled to the side, then drove my boots into his stomach.

He doubled over, gasping. I looked over to see a man in black and gray trying to unhook the chopper. I leaped over Terence and tackled the man to the ground. More men climbed onto the boxcar from the rear of the train. Jet threw off two, ducked under a wild swing, and swiftly took down two more.

A click sounded behind me. I glanced back in time to see Terence release the hook. He grinned as the cable swung free. Air currents pounded down on us from the blades. I squinted up and my heart slowed at the sight of a form bound and gagged in the chopper.

The cable swung past. I grabbed for it. My hands closed around the metal and my breath caught as I was swept past the train in a quick jerk. The helicopter dropped, then rose, trying to shake me off. I climbed quickly. My hands slipped once as the burns and the knife in my arm threatened to steal my control, but I gritted my teeth against the pain and continued climbing. Bullets whizzed past from the men on top of the train. I ducked when one flew by my ear.

Someone tried to slide the helicopter door shut before I could reach it. I grabbed the landing skid and flung myself up to the door. Four men in black and gray and wearing headsets stared at me. Jaze sat on the floor between them battered and bruised. He met my eyes, his own clouded with pain.

Recognition flashed in them. One of the men aimed a pistol at my forehead.

I hit his arm to the side and slugged him in the nose. He pulled the trigger convulsively and the bullet hit the pilot. The helicopter gave a jolt. The pilot slumped forward in his seat and the helicopter tilted forward. Shouts of alarm sounded from the men.

I grabbed Jaze and jumped. The slow-motion sound of the blades cutting through the starlit air echoed around us. Figures fought on top of the boxcars. I recognized Vance's large stature. A detached voice in the back of my mind noted that someone had freed the rest of the werewolves.

I turned to take the brunt of the force just before we slammed on top of the metal surface. We rolled against one of the ribs and pain laced through my shoulder where the knife still stuck out. The helicopter hit the ground next to the train with a tremendous crack; a surge of smoke and flames enveloped the boxcars, then was left swiftly behind.

Forms converged on us. Light from the rising moon lit the top of the boxcars in shades of black and gray. The landscape sped by as the freight train hurdled through the valley. The stars winked down impassively on the chaotic scene on top of the train.

Jaze blocked a blow with his bound arms, then kicked the man's legs out from under him and hit him in the head with his handcuffs. I caught an elbow in the ribs, backhanded my attacker across the jaw, and followed it with a straight punch to the same location. The man turned completely around and collapsed to the roof. A punch caught me in the back. I horse-kicked a werewolf in the stomach with my cowboy boot, then slammed a hammer-fist to the side of his head.

I turned back to see Terence level a gun at Jaze's head. Another werewolf from Terence's pack held Jaze still, his arms bound in front of him and a trickle of blood running down the side of his face from a fresh wound. Jet ran toward us, but he was at the other end of the boxcar and wouldn't reach Jaze in time.

"This is for Trella," Terence said. His finger tightened on the trigger.

I ripped the knife from my shoulder and threw it. It sunk deep into Terence's wrist, knocking the gun from his grasp. He screamed, his wounded wrist clutched in his other hand. He turned to look at me, missed his footing on one of the ribs, and fell from the train.

Jet laid out the werewolf who held Jaze with an elbow to the face, then caught his friend before he could fall. The other werewolves from Jaze's pack took down the rest of the armed humans. The werewolves from Terence's pack who saw their leader fall jumped off the side of the train after him.

"Where's Nikki?" Jaze asked with strength in his gaze that held despite his beaten condition.

"Below, with Taye," Jet said. Relief showed on both of their bruised faces.

My legs felt like they would give out at any second. I wondered if it was from the effects of the silver blade.

"Easy now." I smiled at the voice. Hands that were stronger than they looked helped me to a sitting position on the roof.

Gem watched me worriedly, her expression so different from the smile I was used to that I couldn't help the slight smile that rose to my own lips. "We did it," I said.

Her familiar smile answered. "We did." She threw her arms around me and hugged me tight. "That was amazing," she breathed in my ear. Her warm breath sent a tingle down my spine. I held her close, amazed that we had survived.

"Send Jet to stop the train," Mouse said in my ear.

"Jet," I called. "Mouse wants you to stop the train." He ghosted past me and a few seconds later the train started to slow. Gem tore a strip of cloth from the bottom of her shirt and wrapped it tightly around my shoulder.

"You need to get that looked at." I turned to see Jaze watching us, pain in his eyes but a weary smile on his face.

"Look who's talking," I replied.

He glanced down at his battered condition and shrugged. "It could be worse." He met both of our eyes, his gaze direct. "Thank you. What they wanted from me would have been worse than death."

The things Jaze had told me about his past were horrible; what his captors had planned would have been far beyond that. Gem gave him a quick, gentle hug, then skipped over the ribs to the edge of the boxcar as if we weren't standing on a train that had nearly cost us our lives.

The train eased to a stop near a flat expanse of land dotted by twisted trees. The werewolves and humans we had saved climbed out onto the dusty, midnight ground.

"Jaze?" a voice called.

The love and release that swept across Jaze's face made all of our efforts worth it. He jumped from the boxcar as if his injuries were erased by the sound of Nikki's voice. He swept her into his arms, then pulled his mother close and hugged her as well.

"I'm so glad you're both safe," I heard him whisper above the sounds of the others hugging and laughing.

"I need to get me one of those," Mouse said in my ear.

"A mother or a girl?" I asked.

"Both," Mouse replied. He laughed. "But my grandma wouldn't know what to do with herself if I wasn't there to cook for."

"From what I've seen, you could eat more," I replied.

He laughed again. Gem's arm slipped through mine and we watched them from the top of the boxcar. "So trains, huh?" she said.

I looked down at her and smiled at the way the starlight reflected in her dancing blue eyes. "What about them?"

"Apparently you have a thing for trains. I heard about you pulling that car free."

I laughed. "I think I'll be steering clear of trains for a long time."

She stood on her tiptoes and kissed me on the lips. I leaned down and kissed her back, relishing her embrace and the way her hands held me close, begging me to never let her go. When we parted, she leaned her head against my chest.

"Maybe trains aren't all that bad," I conceded.

She laughed; the light, musical sound enveloped my heart in warmth and peace. I eased down from the train careful of my hands. When I turned to help Gem, she had already jumped down beside me. She laughed at my look. "Werewolf, remember?"

I grinned. "One of these days I'm going to keep up with you."

She slipped under my arm and walked with me to where the others were tending Jaze and Jet's wounds using a medical kit from the train. Nikki cleaned the blood from Jaze's forehead while Taye pressed a butterfly bandage to a gash above Jet's eye. Kaynan and Vance grinned when we drew near.

"You do know how to make a rescue," Kaynan said, looking meaningfully at the smoke that rose from the destroyed helicopter in the distance.

I shrugged. "It's a skill."

Vance laughed. "Remind me to train with you sometime."

"You could use it," Kaynan shot back. Gem laughed

when Vance dove at Kaynan. We left them to their scuffle and made our way toward the others.

Jet rose when we approached. His eyes met mine, calm, direct, but troubled. "I owe you my life," he said quietly.

I shook my head. "It was nothing. You would've done the same."

One of Jet's eyebrows rose. "I laid you out flat the first time we met."

"Jet!" Taye exclaimed.

I laughed. "I was looking for a fight."

"You were trying to survive. It was commendable," Jet replied.

Jaze stared between us. "Commendable?" he repeated with a chuckle. "Jet, what's gotten into you?"

Jet shook his head and pointed at my hands that ached so much I was trying not to think about them. "He burned his hands on my chains to set me free. He could have left me."

"I was tempted," I said with a smile.

Jet shook his head and put a hand on my shoulder, the first time I had ever seen him reach out to anyone other than Taye. "I consider you a brother."

The sincerity and depth to his gaze let me know how much weight his words carried. I nodded, unable to speak. Taye smiled at me with tears in her eyes. "Let's take care of you."

HUNTER

Chapter 16

The dull thud of helicopter blades caught my attention as Taye finished patching up my shoulder.

"The cavalry's here," Mouse said in my ear.

"Mouse sent backup," I told the others.

Jaze gave a relieved nod. "Good, because I really don't want to deal with clean-up right now."

Three helicopters landed a short distance away, and soon a line of SUVs followed the tracks to our position. Jaze walked to meet them, any sign of his injuries erased from his gait and stance. Nikki stood next to him, a human girl and a werewolf with more love between them than I had ever seen.

I winced as Taye scrubbed the silver gel from my raw hands. Gem touched my arm, her eyes bright and warm. I felt complete in her gaze. I rephrased the thought about Jaze and Nikki. There was more love between them than I had ever seen with a werewolf and a human, but werewolf to werewolf, they had their match.

I kissed Gem and she smiled against my lips.

"Hold still," Taye scolded lightly. She spread a salve across my palms, then wrapped them both in gauze. "That'll do until they heal." She gave me a stern look. "Don't take the gauze off until they close so you don't get an infection."

"I won't," I promised.

"You know you will," Gem said as we walked away.

I laughed. "Gauze is itchy."

She poked me in the side, then skipped away before I could catch her.

Jaze's mother, Mrs. Carso, met us at the helicopter. "Ready to go?" she asked with a kind smile. "We'll rest at a safe house we have nearby, then everyone will return home in the morning."

Tears burned my eyes at the thought, but I refused to let them fall. "Earlier today I didn't think we'd make it home," I said.

Mrs. Carso's eyes shone in the starlight. "Me, either," she replied. "You made it happen."

"I'll never take home for granted after this, that's for certain," I told her.

Gem watched silently, but the expression on her face said enough. This was the second time she had almost not returned home. To go back was a gift, and we were able to experience it together.

We climbed into the helicopter and I held her close as it rose slowly into the air. I watched Jaze's team as they worked to clean up the mess and herd the surviving guards into the waiting SUVs. I sat back against the chair and closed my eyes. My shoulder gave a slight, welcome throb when Gem leaned against it; I lifted my arm and she ducked underneath. I pushed away the pain, fear, and adrenaline left from the fight and enjoyed the warmth that spread through my body at her nearness.

HUNTER

***

We reached Jaze's safe house before the others; the rest arrived just before sunrise. Soon, the only sound heard was the quiet tread of the werewolves and Hunters who kept sentry over the house while we slept.

I awoke the next morning to find the pain in my shoulder and hands had vanished to leave only the minor pang of reminder that I was still healing. The skin of my palms was black like the scars on Gem's body, but it only throbbed in a vague memory of the dangers of last night. Much of the weariness was gone from my limbs even though my body was bruised as if I had battled a rhino.

Gem and I slept on the floor in the living room; waking to find her nestled against my side made me not want to move for the rest of my life. All too soon, she took a deep, awakening breath and lifted her head to look at me.

"I thought it was all a dream for a moment," she said with a touch of regret in her voice. She touched the healing scars on my hands. "It's a scary reality to wake up to."

I caught her hand in mine and held it against my chest. "We survived, and Jaze and the others are alright. That's the important thing."

Gem nodded, but a slight shiver ran through her and I pulled her close. "I just wish people would leave us alone to live our lives."

I nodded. "Life was so simple before you came along."

She grinned and pushed my shoulder with a light laugh. "Simple and boring, you mean."

I agreed completely. "I wouldn't trade meeting you for the world."

She smiled and settled back against my chest. "I'm glad."

A scent wafted from the kitchen and I took a deep breath. "I think they're making French toast."

"Mmmm." She sat up. "That sounds wonderful."

She pulled me into the kitchen after her and we found Mrs. Carso and Taye cooking French toast, bacon, and scrambled eggs. Nikki set the table with two humans I assumed to be her parents. Everyone looked clean and fresh after a good night sleep and a shower. It amazed me that we had survived the train yesterday. It felt like a dream in the face of French toast and a set table.

"Looks like you made enough to feed a small army," I said; I accepted the piece of bacon Nikki handed me with a grateful smile.

"Or Jet," Mrs. Carso replied.

The others laughed and Nikki's mom nodded. "That boy's never full."

"Is he up yet?" Gem asked.

Taye shook her head and glanced toward the hall. "He's still asleep. He needs as much rest as he can get."

I thought of his battered face and the fact that he was guarded by six guards alone in the cargo box. It was a lot of work to keep one werewolf under control, but then the memory of him taking down guards one after another on top of the cargo boxes sent a shudder through my skin and I agreed with them. I would hate to be on his bad side.

Taye looked at me, her blue-gray eyes concerned. "How are you feeling? Jet said he wouldn't be here if it wasn't for you."

"Jet saved my life on more than one occasion," I replied grimly. I rubbed my shoulder and gave a small smile. "But I'm feeling a lot better than I was last night."

Mrs. Carso came around the bar and gave me a gentle hug. "Thank you for everything," she said. She then turned to Gem and did the same. "You guys were so brave."

"Very brave," Nikki's mom echoed, hugging me as well.

HUNTER

Nikki joined her and was quickly followed by Taye so that Gem and I were caught in the middle of a group hug. I patted their backs awkwardly and Gem gave me a beaming smile over Mrs. Carso's shoulder.

***

Mouse flew us home. Mom, Dad, Greg, and Anna met us at the tiny Thistle airport. Mom and Dad watched me anxiously as if worried I was going to fall over at any moment. I decided I could probably use some more sleep.

I sat in the back seat wedged between my mother and Gem with Anna on Gem's other side. Mom looked like she wanted to cry when Gem made me lift up my sleeve and show her the healing knife wound and the burns on my palms.

"They're almost gone," I told her.

She studied the new black skin suspiciously. "Are you sure they're not infected?"

I laughed. "I'm not sure werewolves can get infections."

"Unless silver is involved, which was the case," Gem put in helpfully.

I gave her an exasperated look and she grinned at me.

"You have circles under your eyes," Anna said looking at Gem and I. "You both need more sleep."

"That's something I won't argue against," I replied. I tipped my head back and Gem leaned on my shoulder. I saw only scattered glimpses of the journey between the airport and Gem's house.

Golden light drifted between leaves bathed in the light green of a plentiful summer sun. Mile markers dotted past with a steady rhythm that blurred into one solid line. The car moved slightly under the brush of wind from a passing truck. Gem's pink hair tickled my nose and I smiled at the memory of her kisses.

At one point I tipped my head to find Mom watching me, her brow creased and worry in her eyes. "We're alright," I whispered. Gem made a small sound and tucked her head under my chin. A smile spread across my face. "More than alright."

Mom sat back with her own matching smile. Contentment chased away her concern when our gazes met again. I held out my hand and she took it in both of hers.

As I focused on the passing countryside, I wondered if life could ever be the same. When we stopped at Gem's house and I watched Greg and Anna help her sleepily up the porch stairs to the house, I hoped she would rest without nightmares.

"She shouldn't have to sleep alone."

I hadn't realized I had spoken aloud until Dad replied with a chuckle, "I think she'll be alright."

I met his humorous gaze in the rearview mirror and fought back a grin. "She has nightmares, Dad. I just worry they'll be worse if she's alone."

"Oh, is that all?" he teased.

"Yes," I replied, failing entirely to sound upset. "Get your mind out of the gutter."

He laughed out loud at that and Mom patted my hand. She had refused to climb into the front seat with Dad after the Hawthornes left; after all we had been through, I was happy to have her close by. "I'm glad to know that our Dray has turned into such a thoughtful young man."

I chuckled and let my eyes close as the hum of the familiar road under the tires lulled me to sleep.

***

I crawled into bed the second we reached home, and soon found myself wishing that Gem was beside me. Haunting images from the fight, armed guards hiding in cargo boxes, battered faces bound and gagged in the pitch black of a boxcar, Jet's lethal form in the darkness snaking from man to man and ending lives in quick, silent attacks, and my own hands throwing guards out open doors, wouldn't stop flowing through my mind.

Hours passed and I eventually gave up sleeping. The nightmares made me more exhausted than not sleeping at all. I rose and walked slowly to the kitchen. The sound of Mom's breathing and Dad snoring softly in the next room brought a touch of peace to my heart, but I wondered how I could ever rest easy again knowing what people could do to one another.

I poured a cup of fresh milk from the refrigerator and heard Dad sit up and slip his feet into the slippers Mom always set by the side of his bed. I listened to his feet walk down the hall, then tried to look pleasantly surprised when he appeared.

"Oh, come off it," he said, waving a hand. "I know you heard me from a mile away." His hair stuck up in all directions and the robe he wore looked as tattered as I felt. Mom constantly tried to throw it away, but he always found it before she finished the job. He wouldn't let it go, saying it had been there for him too long to get rid of it like junk.

He pulled up a chair and sat down.

"Milk?" I offered, lifting up the glass pitcher.

He shook his head and motioned for me to keep drinking. I complied and sipped the milk slowly, enjoying the way the cold liquid worked its way into my stomach.

"Can't sleep?" Dad asked. When I didn't answer, he smiled. "If I point out the obvious, I can pretend I understand what you're going through." I smiled and he gestured to the glass in my hand. "Molly gave that today. Good milk; it's been her best season."

I turned the cup in my hand, noting the way the cream of the milk coated the sides like paint. I took another drink and imagined it doing the same to my insides.

Dad sighed and sat back in his chair. He frowned and stared at nothing in particular, his eyes distant. "I don't know if I ever told you about the day we brought you home."

I glanced at him. "No, you didn't," I said, surprised at the direction of his thoughts.

He gave a small, tender smile, his gaze on something in the past. "I don't know why your parents put you up for adoption, but Ma and I have always been deeply grateful to them. It felt like the paperwork would never get done, and the approval process took so long your mom was afraid you would go somewhere else."

He looked at me. "You see, we knew you were meant to be with us. From the second they brought you into the office and let us meet you for the first time, and you took my finger in your little hand and brought me to the corner to show me the blocks, I knew we had something special."

Moisture in his eyes reflected the comfortable kitchen lighting. He smiled a weak smile and ran a hand down his face. "I didn't know how special until you turned seven and changed into a wolf for the first time. We didn't know what to do, but we knew we couldn't let anyone know or they would take you away from us and probably do horrible things to you." His tone darkened and he looked away. "But now, they've done it anyway and I wasn't able to protect you. I couldn't save you from a world where people hurt those who are different. I tried to, but I failed."

I opened my mouth to protest, the pain in his voice

driving a dagger into my heart, but he held up a hand, asking me without words to let him continue. I nodded and sat back in my chair, the cup of milk half-finished and forgotten on the table.

"I can't protect my little boy anymore," he said, his voice tight. "But I can help the strong young man he's grown into see that there is still good in the world." He paused, then said, "Jaze's mother called us when you guys reached the safe house after saving all of them. Your ma cried for hours after talking to her."

I looked at him in surprise. "Why?"

He smiled the gentle smile once more. "Because her son has such love and compassion for others that he was willing to put his life on the line to save someone in need, again." He looked at me. "Your mother is a special person, Dray. She is the one who fought tooth and nail to get you here, and she's the one who did most of the work in raising you. To know that you came out far better than either of us is the best thing that a parent could ever ask for."

Tears broke free and flowed down his cheeks. The sight wrapped my heart so tight in love that it chased the fear, pain, and nightmares from my memories. I wrapped my arms around him and we both cried, me for what I had done and seen, and him for the same things, but for far different reasons.

HUNTER

Chapter 17

It felt strange to go to school and pretend like nothing had happened. My shoulder gave a mild twinge when I moved too quickly, but other than that, the bruises and cuts had vanished to leave only a reminder of how lucky I was to be home. Preston and Scotty were only mildly upset at my explanation of a bad cold. They forgot about my absence quickly with the distraction of the Homecoming game next Friday and the dance that was to follow.

"Go with me to the dance," Gem whispered during English class. She grabbed my notebook and began to doodle on it.

I usually avoided the dances at all costs, but I had never had such a beautiful date ask me. I raised my eyebrows. "Are you really sure you want to see me dance?"

She laughed and Mrs. Moody shot us a chiding look before she turned back to her lecture on Fahrenheit 451. I glanced over at Gem's picture and saw a sketch of a wolf in a poofy prom dress. I chuckled and took my notebook back. "That's about how I'll look," I whispered.

Gem laughed out loud, then clapped her hands over her mouth at Mrs. Moody's second annoyed look.

"I'll go with you," I said quietly. "Just stop getting into trouble."

She grinned and nodded, her eyes bright and a touch of color on her cheeks.

***

"Where are you going?"

I turned to see Gem skipping up in a bright summer dress and bare feet; her pink hair accentuated her naturally red lips in the early morning light. It was the first time I had ever seen her wear anything other than long sleeves and pants. I was so used to the black lash marks across her arms and legs that I barely noticed them; I was just happy to see her so free. "I'm cutting hay. It's supposed to storm next week, so we have to get it drying quickly."

She grinned and hefted the basket she carried. "That's what your mom said, so I made us lunch."

I smiled and took the basket from her, then offered her my arm. She settled her hand near my elbow and walked with me to the tractor.

"What's that?"

"A swather." I pointed to the rotating header. "That pulls the hay into the blades."

"Where are the blades?"

I crouched and showed her the rows underneath the header that looked like serrated shark's teeth.

She nodded appreciatively. "Remind me not to get caught in there."

I helped her inside and she laughed. "Where am I going to sit?"

I sat on the springy tractor seat and patted my lap. She laughed and complied, setting the lunch basket between our feet on the floor. The engine grumbled to life and I lifted the header so we could drive.

"Air conditioning." She reached up and pushed a button. Country music from my dad's favorite station yodeled out. "And a radio. Fancy." She gave me a sideways look. "I thought you farmers used sickles and stand in the sun all day behind your oxen."

I pointed to my head. "That's why I wear the hat."

"I see." She took my hat and tipped it becomingly on her head.

I ran a hand through my hair and smiled. "It looks better on you."

She gave me another teasing, sideways look. "I know."

I filled the swather with farm diesel from Dad's tank, then took us along the bumpy, slow drive to the Back Twenty. We reached the first field and I lowered the header and watched it pull the alfalfa steadily into the blades.

"Do you normally drive so slow?" Gem asked after a minute.

I grinned. "It's a slow tractor. If you go much faster, you miss some of the hay."

"More time for your thoughts?" she teased.

"Something like that," I answered with an embarrassed smile.

She watched me for a minute, her bright eyes twinkling. "What are you hiding, Dray Dawson?"

I laughed. "I sing to myself. It helps to pass the time."

She opened her mouth as though surprised. "The manly Dray Dawson spends his time singing in the tractor?" She flipped on the radio. "This I want to see."

I shook my head. "No way. There's a reason I only sing in the tractor."

"Because you're so good you'll be whisked away to Hollywood?" she pressed with a grin.

"Because they'll shoot me to put me out of my misery," I answered.

She laughed so hard I had to laugh as well. By the time she stopped, her cheeks were flushed and the light in her eyes danced with pure happiness. Before I could stop myself, I pulled her close and kissed her soundly on the lips.

She sat back and stared down at me, the teasing gone and something softer gracing her smile. She ran a finger along my jawline, her touch soft on my skin.

"I'm memorizing you," she said softly. She traced my eyebrows, then down my nose, and lingered with her fingers on my lips.

Warmth spread through my body at her touch. "Why?" I whispered.

She smiled into my gaze, her eyes taking me in, seeing all of me for who I was. I had nothing to hide from her, nothing to protect. She brought down all of my walls and I loved her for it. "Because I love you just the way you are," she said before she leaned down and put her lips where her fingers had been.

The field was forgotten and the tractor header spun slowly. I relished Gem's soft skin under my fingers, how she moved toward me at my touch and ran her hands through my hair in a way that sent shudders down my spine. She was mine and I hers. We completed each other in a way I could never have imagined. Our hearts beat together in a solid rhythm that quickened as the moments passed. I loved her. With all of my being, I loved her and I let her feel that love with every look and every touch. She was my world.

I held her close and kissed her, tracing the side of her face with my fingers as she smiled against my lips. I closed my eyes and memorized her feel, her smell, and the way she completed every beat of my heart.

HUNTER

***

We climbed out of the tractor and I laughed at how little work I had gotten done. I would have some explaining to do to Dad when I got home.

"Now might be a good time to eat," Gem suggested, indicating the sun that sat halfway down the sky. She got the basket from the tractor and spread sandwiches, lemonade, apples, and brownies on a blanket. We sat and ate quietly.

She leaned against me, her presence so familiar I would feel empty without her at my side. I tried to keep the heavy thoughts that crowded my mind at bay, but they pressed me down. "I feel guilty in moments like this." The knot that tightened my chest was a familiar one that had haunted my steps since the train.

Gem looked at me. "You have nothing to feel guilty about."

I shook my head. "I killed men on that train." I stared hard at the ground, seeing their faces and feeling each pulse beneath my fingers. "I ended lives."

"They would have killed you," she pointed out gently. She took my hand and held it in her lap, running her fingers over the wavy black scars left by the silver gel.

I couldn't accept her words. The guilt burned through me fierce and strong. "Who says I deserved to live?" I forced out past my tight throat.

She was silent and when I look at her, the understanding in her eyes reminded me that she had gone through so much more. "I asked myself that every time a werewolf didn't return to the cages at Lobotraz. They were my friends." Her voice fell to a whisper. "I didn't know why I kept going. I didn't know why I was stronger than the others." Her hands tightened around mine and she looked up to meet my gaze. "But I know now."

I blinked back tears, the guilt in my chest almost suffocating me. I needed to know her answer. It felt like I was drowning and only her words kept me afloat. "What do you know?"

She took both of my hands in hers and looked at me, really looked at me. There was no humor in her gaze, no smile lingered on her face. In the depths of her eyes I saw the bare expression of a girl who had been trapped with no hope of escape, no hope of relief from pain and torture. In that moment I saw the truth of her; this tiny girl carried a seed of strength stronger than diamond or steel, stronger than all of us.

"You kept me alive," she said. A shock ran up my spine at the truth of her words, the certainty of her conviction. "I didn't know you, but I knew you were there. You carried me even though we hadn't met yet." Her blue eyes sparked. "Don't feel guilty about these moments of peace because we earned them. We suffered and we fought through things we shouldn't have seen or experienced. We didn't ask to be put in those situations. They weren't our fault. But we survived them and because of that these moments are ours. Don't sully them with guilt or regret. Cherish them because if we had been just a little less strong," her voice caught, but she continued, "Or a little less determined, we wouldn't be here."

She leaned her forehead against my chest. "So many lost their lives," she said quietly. She fell silent, then repeated, "So many lost their lives and we need to live for them. We need to live in these moments, to never let them pass by unnoticed. We can't let the past ruin the present, because we are here for a reason." She tipped her forehead against mine and our tears mingled. "And my reason is you," she whispered.

I pulled her close and held her against my heart that

ached with the truth of her words. I would live for her. I would breathe, eat, laugh, and love for her. She was my heart, my everything. She completed me.

"Who would have thought farming was so insightful?" Gem said, wiping her cheeks.

I shrugged, feeling lighter. "You'll just have to come along more often."

She smiled. "I think I can manage that." She tossed an apple my way. I caught it and took a bite while she gathered up the remains of our lunch. We carried it back to the swather and ate our apples while we cut the hay. I let her drive after the second pass and she enjoyed it, but we eventually switched again because she fit on my lap much better than the other way around.

We finished the third field and walked along the ditch while we waited for Dad to pick us up.

"Why don't we just take the tractor home?" Gem asked. She picked up a rock and threw it in the empty ditch.

"Because I'll be cutting the other fields tomorrow, and," I threw her a meaningful look and she grinned in answer, "Catching up from today. It'd be a waste of gas to drive it back and forth. Besides, it's so speedy." I glanced at her. "Are you really coming back tomorrow?"

A smile spread across her face. "Absolutely." She climbed down into the ditch and I followed along the top. The sun had disappeared behind the mountains, casting the sky in streaks of yellow and gold with deep ruby red at the edges. Wispy cirrus clouds shadowed in rose-hued pink and soft purple gave depth to the darkening night sky.

We walked to the road and sat on the grass beside the ditch to wait for Dad. Gem leaned against me and tipped her face up to mine. I lowered my head and kissed her gently on the lips. My hand traced the soft line from her throat to her jaw and I smiled at her smooth, beautiful skin and the way a blush of pretty red rose to her cheeks to rival the sunset.

"You are so beautiful," I whispered.

She tipped my hat back on my head and smiled up at me. "You're not so bad yourself."

Her gaze glimmered in the fading light. I realized her eyes had filled up with tears. "What's wrong?" I asked gently.

"I just didn't know," she said. Her voice caught and she swallowed, then continued, "When I was at Lobotraz, I almost gave up so many times." She rubbed the black whip scars along her arms self-consciously. I pulled her closer and she leaned against my chest. "I thought Vance was the one who carried me through, but he was already in love with another girl. When we got out and he went back to Nora, my parents could tell I was lost. We moved to Thistle to start over."

She took a breath and looked up at me, her tears spilling over. "Then I met you and I realized it wasn't Vance I was living for, it was you."

My heart caught in my chest. "I will do everything I can to be worth what you went through," I whispered.

Her eyes caught the last light of the sun and sparkled like starlight upon the ocean. "You already are," she said.

My breath slowed as I looked at her and saw everything I had ever wanted in life shine in those eyes. I kissed her and held her in my arms, believing by the way her hand rested on my chest and the patterns she traced gently on my arm with her nimble fingers that she was truly mine as much as my heart was hers. I held her as we watched the sunlight fade from the dark green alfalfa.

HUNTER

Chapter 18

"You're sure you have everything taken care of here?" I asked Dad for the tenth time.

He finished tying the last knot and hauled on the rope to tighten its hold around the bales. He and Jeff, the truck driver from the dairy, both laughed at me. "I've got it," Dad reassured me. "Go get dressed."

I walked grudgingly into the house and looked at the suit Mom had set on my bed. The red tie supposedly matched Gem's dress, but since I hadn't seen it, I could only take Mom's word for it. I looked outside, wondering if there was another way I could stall. When I glanced at the clock, I realized was cutting the time a little close and gave in.

I stepped into the kitchen and tugged at the tie. One side was a lot longer than the other, and I was on my seventh try of tying it. "Oh my," Mom said, "Don't you look dashing?"

I handed her the tie, exasperated. "I'd look better if I could get rid of this thing."

She took it and pulled up my collar, then tied it quickly with the practiced ease of a woman who fixed her husband's tie every Sunday. She folded my collar back down, straightened the tie, then stepped back and looked me up and down. I shifted from foot to foot under her scrutiny, aware that I was running out of time.

"Oh, go," she finally laughed. "And have a great time!" She took the corsage out of the refrigerator and handed it to me. "You look wonderful."

"Thanks, Mom," I said. I gave her a kiss on the cheek before leaving.

Dad met me by the truck. "You're not taking her in that, are you?" he asked, eying my green truck dubiously.

"It's a good truck," I pointed out. "I don't know why

everyone thinks otherwise."

"It looks like a turtle lost a race with a twenty-foot tumbleweed." Dad tossed me his keys. "At least give her a little luxury."

I grinned as I caught them. "Thanks, Dad."

Rain started to fall as I pulled out of the garage. Dad gave me a thumb's up and I was glad we had worked so hard to get the hay up in time. I was tempted to turn off the headlights and drive through the darkening night without them, but I figured a ticket wouldn't impress Gem.

I turned into her driveway and smiled at the sight of Greg and Anna at the window watching for me. Anna waved, then ducked behind the curtain while Greg opened the door. I ran in through the rain and Greg shut the door behind me. "Welcome, Mr. Dawson. I assume your intentions are honorable tonight?"

I glanced up at his tone. He held a straight face for a moment, then a laugh burst out of him. "I don't think I could keep Gem from you if I tried."

I had to agree. The little werewolf pixie had me tied around her finger, and I was alright with that.

Gem skipped down the stairs in her normal graceful, dancing way as Anna ran after her with high heels in one hand and a delicate little purse in the other. Both matched the flowing red gown that fit Gem's every curve and set off the glow in her cheeks. The gown fell to her feet and would rise just above that with the heels, while red sleeves fit tightly to her arms and ended in little diamonds with a loop that slipped between her fingers.

She danced to a stop in front of me and twirled. The dress rose around her knees and she laughed. "What do you think?"

I couldn't help but stare. Despite the beauty of the dress,

the real difference was her hair. She had dyed it black and the contrast made her blue eyes look so beautiful and bright I was at a loss for words. She fluttered her eyelashes at me and I realized I hadn't answered her question. "You look absolutely stunning. If I'd known you were going to look that good, I would have done something with my hair."

She laughed, then stood on her toes and kissed me on the cheek. I brought out the corsage from behind my back; it was made of three deep red roses with baby's breath and dark green leaves to accentuate the color. Gem gasped and held out her hand, looking for all the world like a princess allowing a suitor to bestow a favor upon her.

I slipped it over her fingers and settled it on her delicate wrist, then decided her beauty required me to be foolish. I brought her hand to my mouth and kissed the back of it.

Gem exchanged a grin with her mom and dipped in a graceful curtsy. "My lord."

I bowed and held out my hand. "My lady."

She slipped her hand into mine and we bid her parents farewell, then ran through the rain laughing like young children. I held the door open for her and by the time I reached the driver's seat, I was drenched.

"I should have worn my hat," I said, shaking the water from my hair.

Gem laughed. "It wouldn't have matched your suit."

"Maybe I should have gotten a red one to match your dress."

She smiled and leaned against my shoulder. I drove slowly to school, reluctant to dance but eager for everyone to see my beautiful girl. "Are you my girlfriend?" I asked, then kicked myself for the poor timing.

But Gem made up for it. She gave me a smile and took my hand possessively. "Most definitely."

I grinned and pulled into the parking lot. I put my suit coat over Gem's shoulders and she slipped off her shoes and held them in one hand, then we took off running again. Balloons, crepe paper, and silver stars had once lined a walkway from the sidewalk to the gym, but the rain had battered most of it down and it hung in a tattered disarray that nobody noticed as they tried to save their hair and garments from the downpour.

We stopped just inside the door and brushed what water we could from our clothes. Gem handed me my suit coat back and I hung it with the other wet coats near the door. I led her to the entrance of the gym where Coach Matthews and Mrs. Tamlinson, an Advanced Calculus teacher, greeted everyone. "Welcome, Mr. Dawson and Ms. Hawthorne," the Coach said with a warm smile. "I'm glad you braved the weather to join us this evening."

"We wouldn't miss it," Gem reassured him.

We walked inside and Gem let out a little breath of appreciation at the transformation the gym had undergone. It looked like we had stepped out of a rainstorm into a starlit night, complete with paper trees in the corners and a little walkway with green paper cut for grass and an archway for pictures. White balloons, silver stars, and twirled crepe paper in dark blue, silver, and white covered the walls and hung from the ceiling. Several disco balls reflected light that danced across the floor like tiny stars.

"Dray, Gem!" Preston hurried over with Angela from the drama club. She wore a yellow dress that clashed with his bright orange tie and the orange corsage on her wrist. He shrugged with embarrassment. "She said yellow, I heard orange."

She giggled. "I don't mind."

"You look wonderful," Gem reassured her.

HUNTER

"We'll get you some punch," Preston said. He motioned and I followed him to the refreshments while the girls looked at the decorations.

"Scotty's here with Patricia Parsons," he said, pointing in their direction.

Scotty and his partner were already on the dance floor doing what passed for a ballroom waltz step but really looked like they were just stepping backward and forward again and again. Scotty said something and Patricia laughed. He glanced in our direction and lifted his eyebrows. I gave him a thumbs-up for finally having the guts to ask out the cheerleader he'd had a crush on all year.

We ladled some punch into small, clear cups and carried them back to our dates. Gem sipped hers, then gave me a suspicious look. "Did you spike this?"

I laughed. "I should have thought of that. But I wouldn't put it past someone else."

She nodded and set it on a side table. Angela did the same. A slow song started. "Shall we?" I asked Gem. She gave me her hand and I led her onto the floor near Scotty. Though the song had changed, everyone continued the same shuffling walk back and forth. I twirled Gem and she laughed. "You can dance!"

I smiled. "A little. I just prefer not to."

She pursed her lips thoughtfully. "So what dragged you off to such a deplorable activity?"

"A pair of beautiful blue eyes. One look and I'd agree to anything."

She laughed. "Well good. I didn't want you to miss out."

As we danced, more students showed up until the dance floor was packed. The DJ was in good spirits and entertained everyone between songs. Gem and I eventually took a break to eat some refreshments at a round table covered in a silver tablecloth. I got us some cookies and punch and brought them back to the table, then sat down just as the hair rose on the back of my neck.

"Dray?"

Confused, I turned at the sound of Mom's voice. She and Dad stood near the door of the gym.

I was about to go to them when a scent filled the air. A soft growl lifted my lips, then screams of pain and fear sounded in the hallways around the gym.

"Dray, what is it?" Gem asked, her eyes wide.

"The werewolves are back," I answered. I would never forget their scent. The odor of blood that flooded through the doors with it made me nauseous. I motioned for my parents and they ran to our table. Before I could say anything, the doors from the hallway flew open and four werewolves came in. Two were already in wolf form, and all four had blood on them that was not their own.

More screams sounded on the other side of the gym behind the bleachers; two more werewolves in human form came out. My heart slowed at the sight of Terence with a struggling student in his arms. Blood ran down the side of her neck and her eyes were wide with fear. He whispered something in her ear and she fought back, but he tightened his hold on her and she fell still.

"Let her go," Coach Matthews yelled. He staggered into the doorway where Mom and Dad had entered; his hand gripped his arm and blood flowed from between his fingers.

Terence smiled a cruel, taunting smile. "What are you going to do about it?" he asked. Coach Matthews tried to go after him, but Mr. Andrews grabbed him and pulled him back. Terence nodded. "Wise decision." He turned to the werewolf next to him and said, "Phase."

The werewolf tore off his shirt, then phased for the entire

student body and teaching staff to see. His limbs contorted, his muzzle grew, and gray fur ran up his body until we looked at a huge gray wolf where a man had once been. Students' screams filled the air. The scent of terror clouded my nose as the students pressed toward the back of the gym, but the werewolves who had entered earlier spread themselves out until all of the exits were blocked.

"What do you want?" Principal McCormick asked from near the refreshments. I glanced at him, surprised I had missed him among the students. Fear touched his eyes, but he didn't look panicked like the rest of the room. He walked forward until he was in front of those he could protect. "What will end this?"

"End this?" Terence gave a burst of wild laughter the other werewolves echoed. "There isn't an end to something like this. You've seen werewolves. Now we have to kill you all." More screams rose, high and full of desperation.

Terence's hand tightened on the throat of the girl he held. I looked around helplessly, wondering what I could do to stop it. Gem met my eyes, her own wide and scared. The lights from the disco ball over the round tables reflected in the blue sea of her gaze, reminding me of fireflies at twilight.

"Stop," Principal McCormick demanded. "Let her go. She's a student. She hasn't done anything to you."

Terence raised an eyebrow, but his grip loosened slightly. "You assume so much, Mr. . . . ." he paused.

"Principal McCormick. This is my school and these are my students you're threatening," the Principal replied. His voice barely shook and my respect for him rose greatly.

"Oh, this is *your* school," Terence replied. "Well, for you to be fully accountable for these students, you must be fully aware of whom it is you are responsible."

"What are you talking about?" the Principal demanded.

"Let her go," the DJ said into his microphone. At a look from Terence, he dropped the mic and stepped back.

Terence gave a terrible smile and turned to look at the crowd around us. "I demand that the cowardly werewolf pretending to be a student step forward and take what is coming to him."

My heart turned over. I started to rise, but Gem grabbed my hand. She gave a small shake of her head, her eyes pleading. I glanced at Mom and Dad. They met my gaze, matching expressions of fear and helplessness on their faces.

"No?" Terence said. He looked at the girl in his arms. "Dray, you justify the title of coward if you let this innocent girl die in your stead. I know you're here. I can smell you." He tightened a hand over her throat and she struggled, but he barely moved with the force of her fists battering him. Her eyes widened and she began to gasp for air.

"Leave her alone," I yelled.

"Dray, no!" Gem cried, but I couldn't sit still any longer. "Keep Gem safe," I told Dad, then I left them at the table.

Terence's eyes lit with triumph and he let the girl go, shoving her into a cluster of students by the bleachers.

I crossed the room to meet him; the crowd parted around me as if I had the plague. Adrenaline pounding like thunder in my ears and my vision edged with red. "You've gone too far," I growled. My words echoed through the gymnasium as if I shouted them through the overhead speakers. The students fell into an uneasy silence.

Terence's eyes glittered dangerously. "You brought this on yourself. Let's call it payback for the death of my soul mate, my Trella, who was ripped from my life when Jaze and his pack tried to interfere with our presence here."

A snarl lifted my lips. "You attacked innocent people. You lit the hospital on fire. You hurt people I care about, and you helped terrorists kidnap Jaze and his pack in order to sell them to the highest bidder. No one gets away with that."

A gleam of fierce pride touched his eyes. "I will do anything I want to anyone I want. If you want to argue, then here I am, bringing the fight to you on your turf. And when I'm finished with you, I'll make sure this town never forgets who's in charge."

I phased before the last words were out of his mouth. Students screamed and backed away from me. Terence's eyes widened in surprise, then he phased and met my attack. I lunged for his throat and he dodged to the right, then latched onto one of my back feet. I turned and bit down; my teeth sunk into his shoulder before he could do much damage. He let go and circled, his eyes wild and teeth bared.

Students shrieked in terror. I knew I had to get the fight outside. If I could get the werewolves away from the gym, perhaps I could minimize the number of people they hurt. Maybe those in the gym could lock themselves in and the werewolves out.

I let him bowl me off my feet, then scrambled toward the door as if I realized he was bigger and stronger and I was looking for a way out. He jumped on my back and bit at my neck. I shook to break his purchase, then rolled and jumped back to my feet with a speed that caught him by surprise. I took a chunk out of his side, then danced back before he could retaliate. A glance showed the other werewolves following us.

Terence took advantage of my distraction to try for my throat. His teeth tore into the soft flesh, but I yanked back before he could get a secure grip, leaving him with skin and fur in his mouth instead. He bit at my paws and I leaped back, then pretended to stumble into the door. Terence jumped at me and the force of his momentum knocked the door open and pummeled me through. He followed, a growl of rage in his throat and his eyes rolling wildly.

HUNTER

Chapter 19

I slipped on the tiles of the hallway and his teeth cut a jagged gash down my shoulder, then I turned and jumped at the door that led outside, forcing it open with Terence right behind me. Rain poured in sheets and lightning flashed overhead, lighting the area in split-second bursts that blinded my werewolf eyesight and left me biting at shadows where Terence had been.

Someone flipped on the lights to the back parking lot. The bulbs hummed above and circles of light cut through the starless night. The screams of the terrified crowd that had followed us out of the school echoed across the parking lot. Terence's pack had brought fear into their lives and their terror flooded the air with a bitter scent. Girls sobbed and boys consoled them with voices that trembled. A siren sounded in the distance. Someone had called the police.

The rain that hit the pavement fell with a steady cadence that felt far out of place amid the chaos. I blinked, then Terence slammed into my side. He bit at my ribs and stomach, using his superior weight to hold me down. A whine escaped me and a flicker of fear rose in my mind. I bit at his paws and he stepped back out of the way, his muzzle red and a gleam of triumph in his eyes.

Another wolf bit one of my legs. I turned and tore a chunk of hide from his shoulder before he could get out of the way. Terence growled at the wolf, a low warning that said the fight was between us. He wouldn't allow any interference from his pack; he had a score to settle.

We circled slowly. He lunged for my front paws. I jumped to the side and bit at his neck, but he was fast and left me with only a mouthful of fur. He feinted to the right and I followed, then he cut back and bowled me over with his shoulder against mine. I rolled over completely and was back on my feet before he could pin me.

I dove forward, fainted, then lunged for the side of his neck when he moved to stop me, but he didn't stumble with the force of my attack like I thought he would. Instead, he turned and grabbed my throat in his jaws. It was a side hold, not as strong as if he had reached the front where my jugular was protected only by soft tissue, but his teeth had a good hold and he turned his shoulder, forcing me to my side on the ground. I struggled and felt his fangs sink into the muscles of my neck as he bit down.

Fear blossomed with the blood that ran through my fur. I closed my eyes against the pounding rain and saw what would happen if I died. I saw Terence and his pack run wild through the gymnasium, slaughtering my friends, teachers, fellow students, my parents, and Gem. It would be a bloodbath and nobody would escape. I couldn't let that happen.

Time slowed to a crawl that kept pace with my struggling heartbeat. I heard the students screaming as Terence worked his grip a centimeter at a time toward my jugular. I tried to move, but he was stronger and held me down. His jaws closed tighter. I felt the puncture wounds deepen. My airway closed off and darkness flooded the edges of my vision.

"Dray!" Jaze's voice yelled from across the parking lot. I tried to remember why he was there, but my mind was slow to process my thoughts. I struggled to think, to find a way out. The wolf side of me refused to give in. My instincts demanded that I survive, but my strength was waning; my limbs refused to listen, to fight back.

Panic filled me. I didn't want to die a wolf. I wanted to be human one last time so my parents could remember me as a boy instead of an animal. My wolf side refused to let go; the animal will to survive fought to be heard, but I demanded my body to phase, to obey me and let me die as a human.

The wolven instincts warred with my human will, creating a fierce battle inside my body. A strange feeling surged through my limbs. My heart began to beat a double rhythm and adrenaline flooded my bloodstream. I tried to yell, to protest, but my windpipe was clamped shut by Terence's fangs.

Blue touched the edges of my vision. I fought the phase warring inside me, forcing my body to hold it off. In that brief instant, I saw Gem blue eyes staring into mine, her cheeks flushed and my hat on her head as we kissed in the tractor. "Dray!" she cried. Her voice carried above all the others, stark with fear when I had promised her safety. She was mine to protect.

Her voice awakened the beast inside of me. I rolled to the side, ripping my throat from Terence's fangs. "Gem!" I yelled in a voice that was primal and animal, a roar that banished every other sound.

My paws elongated into partial claws as my body slipped between the wolf form and that of a human. I became a beast of both worlds, not human, not wolf, but trapped in between. Cries from the crowd surrounded me; shrieks and sobs of terror resonated across the parking lot. Terence had hurt so many people. He evoked fear and pain wherever he went, and no one was safe because he would continue to hurt whoever stood in his way.

I lifted a clawed hand and shoved it through Terence's chest. I held him against the asphalt, staring at him as the hatred faded from his eyes and they became dull and glassy. A detached part of my mind said that he wouldn't hurt Gem or her family again. Jaze's pack would be safe, and so would the citizens of Thistle. Terence was dead.

I stared down at him in shock as my mind registered what

had happened. Blood pooled around my fingers buried in his chest, puncturing his heart. I pulled my hand free and stared at the dark liquid that coated the black claws, then shifted my gaze to the werewolves around me. Terence's pack stared between me and the still form of their leader. The crowd around us was silent with shock. Rain fell in a soft patter against the asphalt, a simple sound that felt far out of place within the terror of the night.

Jaze was the only one who moved through the darkness. "Dray, what happened?" He looked from Terence to me, and I saw the reflection of my mixed form in his gaze.

I shook my head. The claws disappeared, what was left of my fur faded back into my skin, and my fangs shortened as I stared down at Terence. My body phased completely from wolf form to human, leaving me exhausted and confused. My chest heaved and my heart pounded. Jaze threw a blanket over my shoulders.

"I'm not sure," I said, staring at my hands that now looked normal but were coated in Terence's blood.

"You just turned into part wolf. I've never seen that before."

I shook my head. "Me either."

He stared at me and I realized the impact of what had just happened. All of the werewolves watched me and the crowd waited in stunned silence. Shock radiated from them in waves. I had harnessed the strength of the wolf but stayed human, something no werewolf that I knew of had ever done. I stared back, shock radiating through my body. I felt strong, stronger than I had before, stronger than an Alpha. If I could channel the aspects of a wolf but not be limited by the animal form, I would never be the weaker wolf again. No one would ever hurt those I cared about.

I backed up slowly. Around me, Terence's pack stared at

their leader's still form. At Jaze's quiet word, his pack dragged them to waiting cars with black tinted windows. Jet was with them, as well as Vance and Kaynan. There were other werewolves I didn't recognize and humans helping them haul Terence's pack into the cars. Hunters, a voice in the back of my mind reminded me. Jaze's human allies were called Hunters.

Gem was at my elbow. "Come on, Dray," she urged. I could see the fear in her eyes that she held at bay. She was so petite, but she was strong enough to calm my pounding heart with her loving smile. Relief that we were both alright filled me. Students and teachers stared at us as we passed, stunned by the sharp contrast of a peaceful school dance turned into a violent bloodbath of creatures from a nightmare.

I climbed into my truck and pulled on some clothes I kept behind the seat. Gem opened the door and climbed in beside me. She straightened my shirt, then kissed me as if she couldn't help herself. I pulled her close and kissed her back, relieved to have her in my arms again and know that she was alright.

"I was so scared," she whispered.

"Me, too," I replied, blinking back tears.

"They won't hurt anyone again, will they?" she asked, the need for reassurance tight in her voice.

I shook my head, my forehead against hers. "Never."

She stared at me, her blue eyes bright. "Are you sure you're alright?"

I didn't know what had happened out there, but I felt more than alright. I felt strong and in control of my life, able to protect her against any who would try to cause her harm. "I'm more than alright because you're safe; no one can hurt you now," I replied.

She let out a relieved breath and picked up a rag from the

floor of the truck. With great care, she cleaned Terence's blood from my fingers, washing them so that I could feel like myself again. When she was done, I pulled her closed and kissed her on the forehead, more grateful for her than I had words to express.

She gave me an understanding smile and opened the door. I followed her out of the truck and her arm slipped through mine; we walked together toward the waiting crowd.

Jaze met us in the empty strip of parking lot that separated us from the wide-eyed, staring students and his team who escorted the werewolves to the waiting vehicles.

"Are you alright?" he asked, watching me carefully.

I let out a breath and nodded. "I am."

"Good," he replied. "We'll talk about what happened later."

"How did you know we were here?" I asked. I was aware of the eyes that watched us, filled with fear and uncertainty that I knew would be impossible to erase.

He gestured toward the cars. "We've been following them since the train, but they caught onto us just before they reached Thistle. When we realized Terence had cut out his tracking chip, we called your house but your dad said you were at a dance. When we got here, you pretty much had the fight under control." He watched me, concern and amazement bright in his eyes.

I shrugged uncomfortably. "I did what had to be done."

Jaze nodded. He tipped his head to indicate the watching crowd. "Looks like we have a bit of a situation to address."

The moment I had put off as long as I could had arrived. I turned slowly to see students watching us from the windows and crowding out the doors. Teachers stood around the perimeter to keep them from crossing onto the parking lot.

I took a calming breath, then walked slowly over to the

edge of the throng with Gem and Jaze on each side. We passed the place where Terence's body had lain, but Jaze's team had already taken care of it. I smelled my own blood mixed with his in the rain. I let out a breath and pushed away the sadness that filled my chest.

Mom and Dad watched me from under a light near the door. Dad gave a worried smile. I couldn't bear to look at the pain on Mom's face. I turned to the students and teachers who met my gaze with mixed expressions of fear and uncertainty. A few students drew back when I neared the crowd. Teachers stepped forward as if to protect their students from danger. Police cars sat near the school with their lights whirling. Officers mixed with the students and several talked to Jaze's pack near the government cars. Two ambulances were being loaded with those who had been hurt by the wild werewolves. I hadn't even heard their sirens.

I felt separate from them, different. I realized my life in Thistle had come to a close. I was a werewolf, and I was prepared to face my future. I gave the crowd a reassuring smile. "I'm sorry for the trouble werewolves have caused in Thistle, but I can honestly say that the only part I've had is trying to stop them. I'll go," I said loud enough so everyone could hear. "We're leaving and you'll never have to worry about this happening again. Thistle is safe."

Gem nodded with tears in her eyes. Dad had an arm around Mom and they both leaned against each other for support. Silence filled the air. Only the sound of the lightly falling rain and the grumble of a werewolf as Vance shoved him into a car cut through the night.

Coach Matthews cleared his throat, his hand clutching his bleeding arm. There was a light of bravery on his face when he crossed to me. "Thank you, Dray. We owe you. Don't be a stranger here," he said, his gaze locked on mine and a no-

nonsense look in his eyes.

I blinked. That was the last thing I expected. A smile touched my lips. "I won't."

He gave me a curious look. "Are werewolves any good at football?"

I grinned. "I'm sure, but it's probably way outside the rules."

"Talk about steroids," Kaynan said from behind me; the other werewolves laughed.

Coach Matthews nodded. "Too bad. You would have been great on the team." He walked over and shook Dad's hand, showing the community that they had helped with the fact that Thistle was safe once more. "Thank you for raising such a brave son. Our city is safer because of him."

Dad met my eyes. "I'm proud of him."

The Coach raised his hands. "Let's call it a night." He and the Principal exchanged a look. "Clean-up will begin tomorrow." Students and teachers began to drift away. I caught several glances and smiled, but there was still uncertainty and fear in their gazes. I was right to leave Thistle. As much as it was my home, they weren't ready for werewolves.

"Dray?" I turned at the sound of Preston's voice. He and Scotty stood together as if bracing each other. Their dates waited a few steps behind them, unwilling to come any nearer.

"It's alright," I said, understanding their fear. "I'm still the same person I was before."

Scotty watched me uncertainly. His expensive rented tuxedo was torn and had a punch stain down one sleeve. His hair stuck up in several places, and for the first time, he acted like he didn't care. "You were always a, well, a. . . ."

I nodded encouragingly. "It's okay, you can say it. I was

always a werewolf."

Preston gave a hesitant grin. "That's why you wouldn't join the football team."

"And why you liked your truck so much," Scotty concluded. At my confused look, he shrugged. "More room to do the whole changing thing."

"Something like that," I replied with a smile.

Preston took a steeling breath, then stepped forward and held out his hand. "Thanks for being such a good friend, and for not eating me."

"You bet, man," I replied.

Scotty laughed and shook my hand as well. "It's going to be a lot quieter around here without you."

"I'm going to miss you guys," I said honestly.

They both nodded. I had a brief impulse to hug them, but I pushed it down with the knowledge that it had taken them courage to confront me at all. "Take care of yourselves," I said.

"You, too," Preston replied.

They turned to walk away, then Scotty paused. "You know, my dad's offer of a car still stands."

I laughed. "I'll think on it."

Scotty nodded. "You do that." He slipped his date's hand through his elbow and led her away. Preston and Angela followed close behind. I felt a surge of sadness at seeing them go, but the knowledge that they had each other to lean on made me feel better.

I looked at my parents. They hugged each other, their eyes bright in the starlight. They both looked at me with such proud, shining gazes that I knew everything was going to be alright.

Gem stood near them, beautiful in her red dress with blue eyes so brilliant the stars hid behind the clouds because they knew they were dim in comparison. She gave me a smile so sweet my knees went weak, then she blew me a kiss that landed somewhere on my soul, chasing away the fears and expectations of the future, and leaving only the present.

HUNTER

Chapter 20

I woke up early and watched the sun rise slowly over the farmlands. Reaching beams touched the alfalfa and corn in shades of deep meadow green and sunflower orange. A part of my soul belonged to this land, to the fields I had worked at Dad's side, to the mountains in the distance and the playful breeze that brought with it the scent of morning dew and rich soil.

I took a deep breath and held it, memorizing the way the fresh air filled me completely and cleared the remnants of sleep from my mind. I let it out slowly.

Footsteps sounded behind me. I recognized them and nodded.

"Time to go," Jaze said quietly. I turned back to see my parents waiting by the helicopter, their arms around each other and accepting expressions on their faces. Gem poked her head out of the chopper. She waved at me excitedly.

I took one last look at the fields bathed in early morning light, then crossed to my family. A part of me belonged to the fields, but the girl who shared my soul watched me with dancing blue eyes and a heart-stopping smile. As I waved farewell to my parents, her hand slipped into mine. I watched the farms fade away in the distance and felt the rightness of it all. I was a werewolf, and though the future was uncertain, I would face it with the love of my life, my Gem.

CHEREE ALSOP

About the Author

Cheree Alsop is the mother of a beautiful, talented daughter and amazing twin sons who fill every day with light and laughter. She married her best friend, Michael, who changes lives each day in his Chiropractic clinic. Cheree is currently working as an independent author and mother. She enjoys reading, riding her motorcycle on warm nights, and rocking her twins while planning her next book. She is also a bass player for her husband's garage band.

Cheree and Michael live in Utah where they rock out, enjoy the outdoors, plan great adventures, and never stop dreaming.

Check out Cheree's other books at www.chereealsop.com